GENDER INEQUALITY IN INDIA

GENDER INEQUALITY IN INDIA

Mamta Mehrotra

PRABHAT PRAKASHAN

Published by
PRABHAT PRAKASHAN PVT. LTD.
4/19 Asaf Ali Road,
New Delhi-110 002 (INDIA)
e-mail: prabhatbooks@gmail.com

ISBN 978-93-5048-362-6
GENDER INEQUALITY IN INDIA
by Smt. Mamta Mehrotra

Edition
2025

Price
₹ 250.00 (Rupees Two Hundred Fifty only)

Printed at
Print Media, New Delhi

This book is dedicated to my father late
Sh. P.N. Khanna who brought
me up to be a proud young woman.
He never made me feel that
I belonged to the inferior gender.
I owe all my values and confidence to him.
Whatever I am today is just
because of his courage and values.

Foreword

One Step to Establish the Status of Women

Numerous books in different languages have been published in India and abroad, dealing with the status of women,their problems and solutions.Besides factualbookson women's issue, many literary writers have written on the status of women in the family, work place and society. While feeling,expressing and describing the pain and struggles of women, they have also narratedthe story of achievements of Indian women.

According to the writers and activists,in the past Indianwomen wereoutstanding,but the present situation of women is not good. One finds two setsof views about the status of women in Indian History. There is a group of activists and writers who believe that the past history of Indian women was not good and while searching the ways to emancipate women we must forget the past. Theseare the groups who strongly believe in women'sliberation. They strongly propagate that Indian society is male dominated. Women should be liberated from the domination of men. They should be given their due. Another group of activists and writers believe that we cannot think or read of women's status and problems without men.

We should not blame male dominated society for all the problems of women. The unavoidable situations of the times are equally responsible for the deterioration of the status and persistence of women's problems. The first group of thought totally rejects the glorious past of Indian women. Both the groups differ in the explanations of epics, tradition and different Dharmshstras also. They are of the view that the present problems of women are the outcome of her past.

It is good that the writer of this small, but important book 'Gender' without wasting her time in comparison and conclusion of both groups of activists, has concentrated her efforts to put the facts, and efforts of society, law makersand government to understand andfacilitate the understanding of 'Gender'. The book contains only 108 pages and eight chapters.

The first chapter 'Gender' reveals the intention and purpose of the writer. As an educationist and social activist, she has tried to educate the readerwith the actual meaning and perspective of 'Gender'. After readingjustthe first chapter of the book, the reader can feelthat while talkingin favour ofwomen, the writer does not meanto talkagainst men. She has explained 'Gender' in a widerperspective.

In the remaining seven chapters of this book the writer has clarified issues pertaining to women such asthe status of women in Indian society, gender equality, women and law, Eve-teasing and sexual harassment at work place. One can say that this book is the outcome of the recent episode of gang rape in Delhi, but that is not the truth.

The book is very informative for women activists and concerned section of society, whowish to know every aspect of women in brief. The language is very simple. The writer is free from 'biases'. This is the main specialty of the book. She has put the things as they are. Of course, she has done justice to the objective of writingthe book.

My congratulations and blessing sare with the writer. Waiting to see and readanother valuable book by her.

With blessings

—Mridula Sinha

Author's Note

This book is a very small endeavour on my part towards the realization of my womanhood. I was not born in a conservative family or had a deprived childhood but still at every step was made to feel that I was a woman, the inferior gender.

There was tremendous pressure on me as a daughter, wife and mother. I know I share this tension and pressure with my fellow women. All of us are lonely in our world dictated by the dictums of social gurus. Even if our families wishto give us more liberty and equality, questions are hurled and eyebrows raised by these self-acclaimed custodians of society. Such hypocrites know how to interfere in the personal and family life of others. They are competent to make laws which could shatter the dreams of lakhs of Indian women in the name of society, culture and sanskars. I am sure most of them have not even read a small part of our religious texts,for thenthey would be advocating women's empowerment.

The status of women is how the society perceives a women and not what it should be. Women at every stage are deprived of opportunities because of their sexuality. This book is a small step towards the realization of the fragrance called woman and to accept the Kasturithat is the inherent qualityof a woman.

India is our motherland and we belong to it. It is high time that we learn to give our women respect and treat them with dignity they deserve. Women are the pillars of any society and the foundation stone of any family. Now they should be accepted as such with all their innate abilities, talents, qualitiesand more than that as 'Women' - a wonderful creation blessed with the power of creation and the power to reproduce and replicate; a right and blessing bestowed by nature only on woman for she is the fairer sex - a wonderful creation worthy ofsalutation.

I hope any small step towards the realization of this concept would bealong step in changing the mindset of all our self-acclaimed social gurus and custodians of dharma and fatwas in treating women as equal partners in the growth of the nation, family and children -- an asset which cannot be treated lightly.

—Mamta Mehrotra

Contents

1
Gender

Gender in itself is a grossly misunderstood word. The moment this word is spoken, one arrives at the concept of weaker sex present in society that is the female.

Gender is range of characteristics used to distinguish between males and females, particularly in the cases of men and women and the masculine and feminine attributes assigned to them. Depending on the context, the discriminating characteristics vary from sex to social role to gender identity. Sexologist John Money for the first time in 1955 introduced the terminological distinction between biological sex and gender as a role. Earlier, it was not so common to use the word 'gender' to refer to relative statutes of men and women but use the word only grammatically. However, Money's meaning of the word did not become widespread until the 1970s, when feminist theory embraced the distinction between biological sex and the social construct of gender.

Today, the distinction is strictly followed in some contexts, like feminist literature, and in documents written by organizations such as the World Health Organization (WHO), but in most contexts, even in some areas of social sciences, the meaning of gender has expanded to include 'sex' or even to replace the latter word. Although this gradual change in the meaning of gender can be traced to the 1980s, a small acceleration of the process in the scientific literature was observed when the Food and Drug Administration started to use the word.

While the social sciences quite frequently approach gender as a social construct, partially in regard to gender studies and results do, research in the natural sciences investigates whether biological differences in males and females influence the development of gender-related distinction in socio-economic and political aspect in human. Society and relation both call for debate about how far biological differences influence gender identity formation.

Thus, we should use the word gender as behaviour pertaining to each sex which is socially, religiously and culturally constructed.

The word 'Gender' refers to the different values, attitudes and behaviours that are attached to the roles of males and females by different social and cultural groups. For example, women cook and clean, men fix cars and fly airplanes! Women take care of children and household chores and men are supposedly the breadearner in the family.

Roles of Boys and Girls

Even young children differentiated as boys as girls are, more often than not treated differently. In almost all communities looking at colour taboos and social sanctions, boys are groomed to like masculine colours like blue and not in pink as it is considered to be a 'feminine' colour.

Stereotypical gender roles like males should be tough and females are the weaker sex originates from roles that are taught during childhood. The modern psychology believes that by the age of three, children tend to be aware of their gender. Boys and girls, not exceptionally, are encouraged to prefer the games, clothing, hobbies and part times way of speech, and other aspects of culture usually associated with their sex. Boys are invariably in told "Boys don't cry" and are encouraged to play with guns and other games like cars as toys and girls are given dolls and playhouses and kept indoors, so that they can play the traditional female home-making role and remain submissive. Both the sexes, since childhood, are trained to behave is a particular fashion on the guideline laid down by the society.

The thrust of the traditional family thus has been to make girls schooled to be tender and submissive while boys are groomed to be tough dominating and decision-making. Thus, subtly therefore the society knowingly ingrains the specific future roles and ensures that girls and boys are supposed to play, when they grow up into women and men.

Definition of Gender

(a) "Gender is determined socially; it is the societal to male and female. Each society emphasizes particular roles that each sex should play, although there is wide latitude in acceptable behaviours for each gender."

(b) "Gender is used to describe those characteristics of women and men which are socially constructed, while sex refers to those which are biologically determined. People are born female or male but learn to be girls and boys who grow into women and men. This socially ingrained behaviour makes up gender identity and determines gender roles."

(c) "Gender is the division of set of individuals into subsets, as 'men' and 'women' through interaction with guardian caretakers and the socialization process in childhood. Peer pressure in adolescence, and gendered work and family roles, women and men are socially constructed to be different in behaviour, attitudes, and emotions. The gendered social order is based on and maintains these differences."

Thus, we see that basically gender is not about the two sexes that is male and female but more so how they should behave & the role either sex should be performing socially.

Gender Identity

Gender identity is the gender a person self-identifies as. One's biological sex is directly tied to specific social roles and expectation. The concept of being a woman is considered to have more challenges, due to society not only viewing women as a social category but also as a felt sense of self, a culturally conditioned or constructed subjective identity. The term 'woman' has chronically been used as a reference to and for the female body; this usage has been viewed as controversial by feminists, in the defilement of 'woman'. There are qualitative analyses that explore and present the representations of gender, feminists challenge the dominant ideologies concerning gender roles and sex. Social identity refers to the common identification with a collectivity or social category which creates a common culture among participants concerned. According to social identity theory, an important component of the self-concept is derived from memberships in social groups and categories; this is demonstrated by group processes and how inter-group relationships impact significantly on individuals' self-perception and behaviours. The groups to which people belong will therefore provide their members with the definition of who they are and how they should behave in the social sphere.

Categorizing males and females into social roles creates binaries in which individuals feel they have to be at one end of a linear spectrum and must identify themselves as man or woman. Globally, communities interpret biological differences between men and women to create a set of social expectations that define the behaviours that are 'appropriate' for men and women and determine women's and men's different access to rights, resources, power in society and even health behaviours. Although the specific nature and degree of these differences vary from one society to the next, they typically favour men, creating an imbalance in power and gender inequalities in all countries.

Western philosopher, Michel Foucault, claimed that as sexual subject, humans are the object of power, which is not an institution or structure, rather it is a signifier or name attributed to "complex strategically situation". Because of this, 'power' is what determines individual attributes, behaviours, etc. and people are a part of an ontologically and epistemologically constructed set of names and labels such as being female characterizes one as a woman, and being a woman signifies one as weak, emotional, and irrational, and is incapable of action of actions attributed to a 'man'. Judith Butler said that gender and sex are more like verbs than nouns. She reasoned that her actions are limited because she is female. "I am not permitted to construct my gender and sex willy-nilly," she said. "This is so because gender is politically and therefore socially controlled. Rather than 'woman' being something one is, it is something one does." There are more recent criticisms of Judith Butler's theories which critique her writing for reinforcing the very conventional dichotomies of gender.

The terms 'sex' and 'gender' are often used interchangeably in everyday life but in sociological literature they are frequently differentiated. The term "sex" is applied to differences between men and women that are based on biological differences such as anatomy, physiology, hormones and chromosomes, and in this respect people are female or male.

The term 'gender' is applied to the cultural aspects of male and female roles. In other words, the behaviour, personality and other social attributes that are expected of males and females, and these social attributes become the basis of masculine and feminine roles. Sexuality and the different capacities of men and women in the reproductive process are particularly likely to be thought of as giving 'natural' reasons for gender divisions in society.

A man should always wear pants and shirt and not *saree* for he identifies himself as being masculine and it is but natural for a man to be dressed up in that particular dress code.

A young girl learns cooking from her mother or elderly ladies in the house for she identifies herself to be female and it is but natural for females to know cooking. Though all the *Halwais*, Chef, Buttler cooks are mostly men, yet a female is identified with cooking. For in every family this role is accepted to be female domain.

Thus, from gender acceptability comes gender identity and this define the gender role a particular sex has to play in the society.

Social Categories

Sexologist John Money coined the term gender role in 1955. "The term gender role is used to signify all those things that a person says or does to disclose himself or herself as having the status of boy or man, girl or woman, respectively. It includes, but it is not restricted to, sexuality in the sense of eroticism." Elements of such a role include clothing, speech patterns, movement, occupations, and other factors not limited to biological sex. Because social aspects of gender can normally be presumed to be the ones of interest in sociology and closely-related disciplines, gender role is often abbreviated to gender in their literature.

Most societies have only two distinct broad classes of gender roles, masculine and feminine, that correspond with the biological sexes of male and female. However, some societies explicitly incorporate people who adopt the gender role opposite to their biological sex. For example the Two-Spirit people of some indigenous American peoples. Other societies include well-developed roles that are explicitly considered more or less distinct from archetypal female and male roles in those societies. In the language of the sociology of gender, they comprise a third gender, more or less distinct from biological sex (sometimes the basis for the role does include intersexuality or incorporates eunuchs). One such gender role is that adopted by the *hijras* of India and Pakistan. Another example may be the Muxe (pronounced as mufe), found in the state of Oaxaca, in southern Mexico, "Beyond gay and straight".

The Buggies people of Sulawesi, Indonesia have a tradition incorporating all of the features above. Joan Rough Garden argues that in some non-human animal species, there can also be said to be more than two genders, in that there might be multiple templates for behaviour available to individual organisms with a given biological sex.

Along with male and female and erogynous come to occupies a role in their exiting society. With the concept of gay and lesbian rights increasing in much society gender identity could be further decided in the coming time.

❐

2

Status of Women in Indian Society: A Socio-historical Perspective

For a sociological understanding of women's status, it is important to keep in mind social institutions such as class, caste, family marriage and kinship in rural and urban India.

In the year 1950, the Constitution of India came into existence. It not only declared that men and women are equal, but also prohibited any kind of discrimination against women. Yes, it is true that our Constitution provides that men and women should have equal opportunities. The movement for gaining equal opportunities has a history of more than two centuries. Due to the efforts of social reformers, women's movements and the Constitution of India, hurdles to women's liberation have been removed. But, in reality, the obstacles to the emancipation of women have not all been eliminated. This is because, many of the problems, which women have been facing, are not yet solved. Women have been facing problems for several centuries.

With the help of available sources of information, we can try to construct a picture of the way the status of women saw ups and downs during different periods of history.

In fact, tracing the status of women in India from a historical perspective is not an easy task because systematic documentation (records of facts) on the position of women in different social groups at different points of time began only recently. Using authentic (reliable) sources of information an attempt is made in this lesson to analyse the status of women during different periods of history. We have divided these into three major periods: Ancient, Medieval and Modern.

Status of Women During the Ancient Period

Status of women during the ancient period is presented under four broad sub-periods listed below. These, however, do not follow s chronological sequence. Ancient Indians are changed with a lack of historic sense. They did not write helotry as it is written today.

(i) The Vedic Period
(ii) The Period of the Epics
(iii) The Period of Jainism and Buddhism
(iv) The Age of Dharmashastras

The Vedic Period

The earliest known source of information available about ancient India is the Rig Veda. The period between 1500-1000 B.C. is identified as the early Vedic or the Rig Vedic Period. Though we cannot clearly state that this age was characterized by total equality between men and women, it is evident from available data sources that many liberal attitudes and practices pertaining to women existed during this period. Women took part in religious and social activities and they had some freedom to choose their life partner in marriage. Marriage was not compulsory for women. The daughter was not considered a liability or an unwelcome guest in her parental household. Girls would also be initiated into Vedic studies.

The Rig Vedic Aryans were patriarchal. The position of husband was considered superior to that of his wife. Polygamy was permissible. A widow was permitted to marry as is demonstrated by the prevalent practice of a widow carrying the younger brother of her deceased husband. In short, it can be said that to an extent women in the early Vedic period lived in liberal social atmosphere.

The Period of the Epics

Dated broadly to 3139 B.C., *Mahabharata* is newer than *Ramayana* dated to 5th century B.C. Do not we all know the story of Ramayana and Mahabharata? The two great epics, *Ramayana* and *Mahabharata* have played key roles in moulding (shaping) the ideology (beliefs) of Hindus as well as their attitudes towards women. It thus becomes important to discuss the portrayal of women in the two epics when we are discussing the status of women. The two great epics, *Ramayana* and *Mahabharata,* have a strong influence on Hindu Society. Even today girls are being brought up to follow in the footsteps of Sita, the wife of Rama. Sita is considered the ideal Hindu woman because she surrendered all her personal desires and followed Rama to the forest. On the other hand, Draupadi the central female character of *Mahabharata* is a woman who exhibits a greater sense of independence and courage. Sita of *Ramayana* and Draupadi of *Mahabharata* are well-known today. In spite of their subjugated status vis-à-vis their husbands, they are universally respected and have become role-model. The self-imposed blindness of Gandhari as a mark of respect of her blind husband did not lower her status as a queen. In fact, she gives out the message that a respectable wife is one who humbles herself vis-à-vis her husband. Ancient India's march to civilization was accompained by the growth of social discriminations.

The Period of Jainism and Buddhism

Jainism and Buddhism took roots around the 6th century B.C. Both the religions emerge as potent religious reform movements. The post-Vedic Varna divided society and the ritualistic domination of the priestly class of the Brahmanas led to the emergence of Jainism and Buddhism as protest movements. Jainism evolved as a religion distinct from Hinduism. Though it recognised the existence of the gods, it placed them lower than the Mahavira (Jina). Jainism made the first serious attempt to mitigate the evils of the varna order and the ritualistic Vedic religion. Women were admitted to the religious order and could give up family life to become ascetics. During the time of Mahavira, a large number of women drawn from different backgrounds joined the monastic order. In Jaina Literature, there are references to women who had achieved remarkable success as ascetics. Buddhism did not recognize the existence of God and soul *(atman)*. This was a kind of revolution in the history of Indian religions. It appealed to the common people. It particularly won the support of the lower orders as it attacked the varna system. Buddhism permitted women to participate in religious discourses and seek membership in Sangha. Many women monks composed verses, which came to known as Therigatha.

The high status women enjoyed during the early Rig Vedic period, gradually started deteriorating in the late Vedic period between 1000 and 500 B.C. Women began to be confined to the household. Because of the importance given to values such as purity (ritual cleanliness) and pollution (ritual impurity or contamination), women bagan to be considered impure during certain periods of their life. They were kept away from many religious and social occasions. Lineage began to traced in the male line and sons were the sole heirs to family property. As the economic and social status of sons began to rise, the position of women saw a steep decline. The strong belief of the day was that only a male heir could save his parent from the cycle of rebirth. Since a daughter left her parental home after carriage, it was the son who was left with the responsibility of caring for parents in their old age. This further added value to the sons.

A woman's place was the home and her primary responsibility was to bear sons and ensure the continuity of the family lineage. A husband's rights over his wife were total and he had the freedom to go for another marriage, if his wife failed to beget sons. A woman was kept constantly under male control and lost her right to seek knowledge. Over a period of time, marriageable age was also lowered, though there was a general decline in the status of women in post-Rig Vedic period. Now there were still instances of women intellectuals who showed great scholarship. Gargi and Maitreyi are the most well-known women scholars of this period. There are also references to women studying the Vedas and going through initiation rituals. But by and large the position of women went on witnessing a steady decline and reached an all time low during the age of the Dharmashastras.

The Age of Dharmashastras

During the age of Dharmashastras codes of conduct, which served as the base for prescribing behaviour norms also for women were evolved. These belong to large body of secular literature compiled in 500-200 B.C. This period saw the exclusion (leaving out) of women from both economic and religious spheres. Since education was virtually denied to women, they had to be dependent on men for their survival and maintenance. The concept that women were inferior to men gained ground and women were pushed to a state of utter despair and ignorance. This period was also characterized by consolidation of religious customs and caste system assuming rigid proportions.

The Dharmashastras prescribed codes of conduct, which regulated not only family life but also life in society at large. They also prescribed punishments for violation of these codes of conduct. The two most important authoritative law codes of this period were *Manu Smriti* and *Yagnavalkya Smriti. Manu Smriti* upheld the view that a woman did not deserve freedom at any point of time in her life ("Na Sthree Swathanthram Arhati"). Manu's view was that a woman, in her childhood is dependent on her father, in her youth on her husband, and in her old age on her son'. This view of Manu was not just a theoretical idea but also a practice followed *in toto* by the society of that period. The same Manu also said that "where women are respected, there the God's delight". This is a statement, which is in clear contradiction of his pronouncements about women not deserving any freedom.

Yagnavalkya laid down that parents who did not get their daughters carried before they attained the age of puberty would be committing an unpardonable sin. The Dharmashastras planted the impression that an unmarried woman could never attain salvation from worldly obligations if she remained single. As a result, carriage came to be considered an unavoidable ritual for a woman. While girls had to be carried at a very tender age, no such restrictions were imposed on men. The husband was even given the right to enforce the obedience of his wife by resorting to physical punishment.

During the period of Dharmashastras, child marriage was encouraged and widow marriage looked down upon. The birth of a girl came to be considered an ill omen and many parents went to the extreme extent of killing their female infants. The practice of *Sati* became quite widespread because of the ill-treatment meted out to widows.

It was during the period of the Dharmashastras that the status of women completely deteriorated. Women led a life of total subjugation (subordination) and had virtually lost all hopes of emancipation (freedom). This situation more or less continued until the 19th century when the social reform movements launched a struggle to improve the conditions of women.

The Medieval Period

The 11th century saw the emergence of Islam, which created hopes of promoting the interests of the oppressed groups, but also introduced certain values and practices, which did not help to enhance the status of women or emancipate them from their bondage. The system of *purdah* (using a veil to cover the head/face/entire body/mostly remaining indoors), which was generally prevalent among royal families, nobles and merchant prince classes prior to the advent of Muslims spread to other classes also. These customary practices of the upper castes, particularly the twice born castes were considered as the practices of all Hindus. The lower castes gradually adopted upper castes' customs. The strict observance of *purdah* resulted in the seclusion of women from men who did not belong to their family and also the world outside.

Marriage was a contract among the Muslims and it was a man's prerogative to divorce his wife. In a system, where there was no provision for payment of alimony (maintenance after divorce), the wife was left to fend for herself. Among the Muslims marriage, divorce or inheritance questions are decided as per the provisions contained in the Muslim Personal Law (Shariat). Even today, in the absence of a uniform civil code, Shariat governs Muslim family life. The fact that large number of Muslim women have still not been able to access opportunities for education leaves them at mercy of rigid patriarchal values and practices.

During the medieval period, practices such as polygyny (the marriage in which a man has more than one wife), *sati,* child marriage, ill-treatment of widows already prevalent during the Dharmashastra Age gained further momentum. The priestly class misinterpreted the sacred texts to their advantage and created an impression that all these evil practices had religious sanction. Since women were denied the right to education and kept away from participation in home, they could neither know the reality nor question the existing practices.

The Modern Period

The modern period began with the onset of the 19th century. The British came to India in 1600 A.D. For nearly 200 years in their East India Company incarnation there was no real effort made to address questions of social inequality or social oppression. Social evils such as *sati,* suppression of widows, denial of the right to education for women, and child marriage flourished unchecked. With the dawn of the 19th century, an era of change began and it was during this period that many efforts were made both by the British rulers and progressive sections of Indian society to put an end to social evils.

The Modern Age can be classified into two periods. These are:

(i) The British Period (1800-1947).

(ii) The Period after Independence (1947-till date).

Let us start with the British Period first.

The British Period

The British set in motion an era of social reform when they imposed a ban on the inhuman practice of *sati* (the practice of self or forced immolation of a widow on the funeral pyre of her husband) in the year 1829. The famous social reformer Raja Rammohan Roy's fight against *sati* received a positive response from the then Governor General Lord William Bentick who took the lead in enacting the Sati Prohibition Act. Religious fundamentalists and traditionalists put up a stiff resistance to this Act by claiming that the British Government had meddled with a custom sanctioned by religion. But the voices of reason prevailed and the British Government refused to withdraw the Act. However, a distinction was made between voluntary *sati* and forced *sati*. Also, the passage of this Act did not put an end to the practice of *sati*.

Because of the ban on widow marriage and lack of opportunities for education, women who were rescued from the practice of *sati* had to undergo a great deal of suffering. Many widows preferred to die, because life held no meaning for them.

It was this plight of young and tortured widows that moved West Bengal's great reformer Ishwar Chandra Vidyasagar, who led the movement for lifting the ban on widow marriage. Due to his efforts, the Widow Remarriage Act of 1856 was passed. Though there was no significant increase in number of widow marriages, the passage of this Act paved the way for ending longstanding oppressive custom. Social approval of widow marriage was also not forthcoming immediately. Vidyasagar had to often bear the wrath (anger) of hostile fundamentalists, who did not even hesitate to hurl physical assaults on him for his role in lifting the ban on widow marriage. The great scholar and a truly progressive human being that he was. Vidyasagar went ahead with his progressive reforms. The role of Vidyasagar in promoting the cause of women's education also deserves special mention.

The social reform movement, which started in West Bengal, spread to other parts of India too. Jyotiba Phule, the great reformer from Maharashtra, dedicated his life for the cause of women. He started a school for girls in 1848 and in 1852 established the first school for Dalit girls. He also supported widow marriage and started a home for protecting the children of widows. Women's education got a fillip (boost) in Maharashtra from Maharshi Karve who was a pioneer in establishing educational institutions for girls and women. This period saw immense philanthropic (humanitarian) activity by many Indians in different parts of country.

There were also a number of other progressive pieces of legislation during the British period, prominent among these being the Child Marriage Restraint Act of 1929. Many of woes of women were rooted in child marriage. Leave alone child marriage, there were ever infant marriages. The Act of 1929 fixed the minimum age at marriage for girls as 14 years and for boys as 18 years. Harbilas Sarda took the initiative in leading the campaign for increasing the age at marriage and in recognition of his role the Act also came to be known as the Sarda Act. Today the minimum age at marriage for a woman is 18 and for a man, 21 years. These changes were brought about by the Child Marriage Restraint (Amendment) Act, which was passed in 1976.

The pre-independence era of the twentieth century was also remarkable for one more reason. The large-scale participation of women in freedom movement both as visible and invisible freedom fighters was standing testimony not only to their capacities. Gandhiji, under whose leadership women participated in the nationalist movement opposed such practices as child marriage and dowry. "*Swaraj* without social reform was not a meaningful proposition" was Gandhiji's view.

The British period saw the rise of social reform movements which took up the issue of gender inequality, primarily by passing laws that removed barriers to women's emancipation. Though widespread changes did not take place, the stage was definitely set for launching a struggle for creation of a gender just society (a society in which laws give equal treatment to men and women. In cases relating to women courts must give judgments in such a way that the interests of women are protected). Independence brought new hopes and led to creation of departments and launching of schemes, meant exclusively for improvement in the status of women.

The Period After Independence

After India got her independence, the Constitution of India laid the foundation for creating a social order where men and women are treated as equals. While Article 14 of the Constitution conferred equal rights and opportunities on men and women, Article 15(1) prohibited discriminations against any citizen on grounds of sex. The Constitution through Article 15(3) also laid down that the state can make special provision for women. According to Article 16(2), no citizen shall be discriminated against in respect of any employment in office under the state.

The Directive Principles of State Policy prescribed that:

(i) Men and women equally have the right to adequate means of livelihood.
(ii) There is equal pay for equal work for both men and women.
(iii) The health and strength of women workers cannot be abused.
(iv) Provision should be made for securing just and humane conditions of work and for maternity.

A number of laws were also implemented for liberating women from oppressive social customs and protecting their rights. Prominent of these laws are as follows:

(i) The Hindu Marriage Act, 1955 (this Act made monogamy compulsory and created a provision for divorce. It had prescribed the minimum age at marriage as 15 years for a girl and 18 years for a man).
(ii) The Hindu Succession Act, 1956 (This Act confers property rights on women; but the provisions of the Act applied only to self-earned property and equal share is not guaranteed for women in ancestral property).
(iii) The Dowry Prohibition Act, 1961 and the subsequent amendments of 1984 and 1986.

(iv) The Maternity Benefit Act, 1961 (This Act grants maternity leave with full pay for 135 days to women who have completed 80 working days in a given job and prohibits the dismissal or discharge of woman during the leave period. This extends to factories, mines, plantations, shops and establishments where 10 or more persons are employed).

(v) The Equal Remuneration Act, 1976 (this Act provides for payment of equal wages for men and women for equal work).

(vi) The Indecent Representation of Women [Prohibition] Act, 1986 (this Act prohibits indecent presentation of women in advertisements and media campaigns and makes it a punishable offence).

Besides the Acts referred to above, there are also many legislations such as Hindu Adoption and Maintenance Act of 1956, The Immoral Traffic Prevention Act of 1956 amended in 1986, The Family Courts Act of 1984 and The National Commission for Women Act of 1990 have been passed after the country became independent.

Constitutional provisions and a series of laws have actually paved the way for bringing about major changes in the lives of women. Though women have been enfranchised, their age long social subordination continues to prevail in many forms. In the 55 years following India's Independence, the position of women of different indicators of development such as education or life expectancy has improved considerably, but there are still gaps in such areas of access to health care or work participation. There are yet several causes for worry.

Let us start by taking a look at sex ratio. Sex ratio refers to the number of females per 1,000 males. Table 1 will give you information on how many women there were/are per 1,000 men during the different census periods.

India's sex ratio, which stood at 972 women per 1,000 men in 1901, had declined to 927 per 1,000 by 1991. However, in the 2001 Census, there has been only a slight improvement to 933 per 1,000 men. There are also wide variations between different states. Kerala is the only state in India where there are more women than men. The sharp decline in the number of female infants (0-12 months) and girl children (1-6 years) in almost all the states of the country is a cause for concern. Life expectancy at birth for females increased from 23.3 in 1901 to 61.8 years by 1997 and this indeed is a heartening development. Improved access to health care and lower fertility ratios in some states are predominantly responsible for this phenomenon. But this happiness is taken away, when we realize that maternal morality (death of mothers in childbirth) rates have increased from 424 per 1,00,000 live births in 1992 to 540 in 1998. It is estimated that 80,000 women die every year in India during childbirth. The fact that even today only 34 per cent of births take place in medical institutions and lack of access to safe antenatal care are primary causes for death of mothers during childbirth. Early marriage, frequent childbirths, poor nutrition and burden of the household work take a heavy toll on women's health.

Table 1 : Census of India Reports of Different Decades

Census Year	Male	Female
1901	1,000	972
1911	1,000	964
1921	1,000	955
1931	1,000	950
1941	1,000	945
1951	1,000	946
1961	1,000	941
1971	1,000	930
1981	1,000	934

1991	1,000	927
2001	1,000	933
2011	1,000	940

Female literacy increased from 39.42 per cent in 1991 to 54.16 per cent in 2001 (an increase of nearly 15 per cent in a span of 10 years). In fact, it is only during that a visible rise took place in number of literate women. The data in Table 2 will show you that in the 50 years after the country became independent female literacy increased only at a marginal pace.

Table 2 : Literacy Rates in India

Census Year	Persons	Males	Females
1951	18.33	27.16	8.86
1961	28.31	40.40	15.35
1971	34.45	45.96	21.97
1981	43.57	56.37	29.76
1991	52.21	64.13	39.29
2001	64.83	75.26	53.67
2011	74.04	82.14	64.46

Note: Literacy figures for Census of 1951, 1961 and 1971 applied to persons of five years of age and above. From the Census of 1981 literacy percentages are being calculated for persons of seven years of age and above age group.

Sources: NIPCED, Statistics on Children in India, 1992. Annual Report 2001-2002, Department of Women and Child Development, Government of India.

Improved access to education has helped many women overcome the obstacles to their illiteracy. An increasing number of women are now getting opportunities for not only acquiring skills but also enhancing their income earning capacities. In spite of the increase in the percentage of literacy, there are differences among states in making use of educational opportunities. While states like Kerala, Maharashtra, Goa, Mizoram, Tamil Nadu, and many of the northeastern states and the Union Territories have recorded a significant rise in literacy, states like Rajasthan, Jharkhand, are still on lower side. It is also true that school drop-out rates rise sharply in higher primary and high school levels. This is primarily due to the emphasis being given for preparing girls for shouldering family responsibilities. In spite of the programme of free compulsory education being in existence for nearly fifty years, a large number of girls are not able to make use of these opportunities on account of domestic burdens and constraints.

Work participation rates for women are still very low. It is only 23.3 for females as against 57.6 for males. Only 17 per cent of women are in organized sector (those jobs protected by labour laws) employment, while women work in low paid and overworked jobs.

While the law tightens its hold on offenders responsible for incidence of violence against women, in actual practice cases of violence against women are also on the increase. This is indeed a disturbing trend, which cannot be taken lightly. However, it is also true that there is growing awareness among women of their rights and there is a strong women's movement, which has been addressing questions of gender inequality and gender injustice. But the movement for women's emancipation has to touch the lives of larger sections of India's population if there has to be a real change in the position of women.

❐

3

Gender Inequality

The 'set' activities assigned to girls and boys do not end with the selection of toys for each. They even influence the selection of subjects in school and college. Later on, the value attached to the work of males and females also differs.

Most women work much harder than their male counterparts. But the invisibilisation of women's labour fails to get them their due share. The housework and childcare are not considered 'work'.

They are the duties of the woman are rights of man to be tabes care of.

Gender inequality exits in most parts of the world in different forms:

1. Mortality Inequality: Women mortality rates are higher as compared to men all over the world.
2. Natality Inequality: Many male-dominated societies have preference for boys. The techniques of determining the gender of the fetus have encouraged this inhuman practice.
3. Basic Facility Inequality: Girls are denied the right to education and many facilities in many countries, even today.
4. Special Opportunity Inequality: The opportunities of higher education and professional training are less for young women and more for young men.

5. Professional Inequality: In employment as well as promotion, women often face discrimination.
6. Ownership Inequality: In many societies the basic assets, i.e. home and land are owned by males. The lack of claim to property reduces the voice of women.
7. Household Inequality: There are basic inequalities in gender that are reflected in sharing of housework and child care.

Gender Equality

The meaning and content of the fundamental right guaranteed in the Constitution of India are of sufficient amplitude of encompass all the facts of gender equality including prevention of sexual harassment or abuse. Independence of judiciary forms a part of Indian constitutional scheme. The international conventions and norms are to be read into them in the absence of enacted domestic law occupying the field when there is no inconsistency between them.

Gender equality includes protection from sexual harassment and right to work with dignity, which is a universally recognized basic human right. The common minimum requirement of this right has received global acceptance. The International Conventions and Norms are, therefore, of great significance in the formulation of the guidelines to achieve this purpose.

Gender relations need to be measured in the context of participation in and sharing of the important decision-making process that results in the above inequalities. Such a measure would help identify the differing degrees of inequality in terms of age, income levels and geographical location. For governments and concerned citizens seeking to redress these inequalities, indices are a means of determining the issues on which they must concentrate, and provide feedback on the effectiveness of their actions.

Clearly, then the accuracy of any measure of gender inequality needs close scrutiny.

As per the report of review of the New Internationalist's "Women—A World Report", there has been progress in the field of gender equality since 1985, but less than what was expected. The report illustrated how women's ability to bear children means they are expected to take responsibility for domestic work worldwide. A woman in a Pakistani village, for example, spent around 63 hours a week on domestic work alone. But housework is everywhere invisible and undervalued. If the services provided free by a housewife in the USA in 1979 had been purchased with wages at market rates, they would have cost $ 14,5000 a year. On this basis unpaid work done in the industrialized countries contributes 25-40 per cent GNP.

Equality must not remain mere idle incantation but must become a vibrant living reality for the large masses of people. In a hierarchical society with an indelible feudal stamp and incurable actual inequality, it is absurd to suggest that progressive measures to eliminate group disabilities and promote collective equality are antagonistic to and anathema of equality on the ground that every individual is entitled to equality of opportunity based purely on merit mantra judged by the marks obtained by him.

The apex court cannot countenance such a suggestion, for to do so would make the equality clause become sterile and perpetuate existing inequalities. Equality of opportunity is not simply a matter of legal equality. Its existence depends not merely on the absence of disabilities but on the presence of abilities and opportunity for excellence in each cadre/grade. Where, therefore, there is inequality, in fact, legal equality always tends to accentuate inequality. It is, therefore, necessary to take into account *de facto* inequalities which exist in the society and in order to bring about real equality, affirmative action fills the bill and allows to give preference to the socially and economically disadvantaged persons by inflicting handicaps on those more advantageously placed.

Such affirmative action, though apparently discriminatory, is calculated to produce equality in results on a broader basis by eliminating *de facto* inequalities and placing the weaker section of the community on a footing of equality with stronger and more powerful and disadvantaged sections so that each member of the community, whatever is by his birth, occupation or social position, may enjoy equal opportunity of using to the full, his natural endowments of physique, of character and of intelligence.

The principle was approved and reiterated by the Constitution Bench in Marri Chandra Shekhar Rao vs. *Dean,* Seth G.S. Medical College. It would thus a settled constitutional principle that facilities and opportunities should be given to the Dalits and Tribes for promotion to higher cadre or grade, gain accelerated seniority by the Dalits and Tribes and delimit the seniority of the erstwhile general candidates in the lower cadre or grade in accordance with the roster point.

Women in the Military: Equality to Kill (and to be Killed)

Owing to labour shortages during World War II, all military branches were enlisting women by late 1942. Their, entry into and other supposedly traditional male spheres of life triggered considerable controversy. One church argued that the Women's Army Crops was "Intended to breakdown the traditional American and Christian opposition to removing women from the home. By bringing back the pagan female Goddess of de-sexed, lustful sterility".

In the NORC 1982 General Social Survey, Americans were asked whether they think a woman should or should not be assigned as a soldier hand-to-hand combat assuming she is trained to do it.

Percent Men and Women Saying Women Should be Assigned to Combat Roles

Birth Cohort	Pre-1910	1910-19	1920-29	1930-39	1940-49	1950 on	Total
Female	17%	21%	34%	35%	43%	58%	38%
Male	22%	15%	17%	34%	36%	36%	30%

In total, observation in the right – most columns show how women were eight percentage points more likely than men to believe that women should be assigned to combat roles. This total, however, does not reflect some interesting generation dynamics at work. For men, the big divide is between those born before and after 1930 those roughly older or younger than 50 years of age in exercised their right to vote in 1920, and between those born before and after the Korean war. Finally, observe how the sexes most differ in attitude immediately after these generation divides: among those born in the 1920s and in the 1950s. (Not revealed in this table is how support within sexes declined between those born in the 1950s and 1960s, with a nine percentage point decline for women and four for men).

Twelve years after this question was presented to the American public in 1994 President Bill Clinton signed an order allowing women on combat ships and aircraft. Thirteen service women died during the 1991 Gulf War, four from enemy fire, and 21 were wounded in action. In the 2003 Gulf War, women made up one in seven of the military personnel in Iraq.

❐

4

Constitution and Gender

1. CONSTITUTIONAL PROVISIONS

The Constitution of India not only grants equality to women but also empowers the States to adopt measures of positive discrimination in favour of women for neutralizing the cumulative socio-economic, education and political disadvantages faced by them. Fundamental Rights, among other, ensure equality before the law, equal protection of law, prohibit discrimination against any citizen on grounds of religion, race caste, sex, place of birth and guarantee equality of opportunity to all citizens in matter relating to employment.

Constitutional Privileges

(i) Equality before law for women. (Article 14)

(ii) The State not to discriminate against any citizen on ground only of religions, race, caste, sex, place of birth or any of them. [Article 15(i)]

(iii) The State not makes any special provision in favour of women and children. [Article 15(3)]

(iv) Equality of opportunity for all citizens in matter relating to employment or appointment to any office under the State. (Article 16)

(v) The State to direct its policy towards securing for men and women equally the right to an adequate means of livelihood [Article 39 (a)]; and equal pay for equal work for both men and women. [Article 39 (d)]

(vi) To promote justice, on a basis of equal opportunity and to provide free legal aid by suitable legislation or scheme or in any other way to ensure that opportunities for securing justice are not denied to any citizen by reason of economic or other disabilities. (Article 39A)

(vii) The State to make provision for securing just and humane conditions of work and for maternity relief. (Article 42)

(viii) The State to promote with special care the educational and economic interests of the weaker sections of the people and to protect them from social injustice and all forms of exploitation. (Article 46)

(ix) The State to raise the level of nutrition and the standard of living of its people and the improvement of public health. (Article 47)

(x) To promote harmony and the spirit of common brotherhood amongst all the people of India and to renounce practices derogatory to the dignity of women. [Article 51(A)(e)]

(xi) Not less than one-third (including the number of seats reserved for women belonging to the Scheduled Castes and the Scheduled Tribes) of the total number of seats to be filled by direct election in every *Panchayat* to be reserved for women and such seats to be allotted by rotation to different constituencies in a *Panchayat*. [Article 243D(3)]

(xii) Not less than one-third of the total number of offices of Chairperson in the *Panchayat* at each level to be reserved for women. [Article 243D(4)]

(xiii) Not less than one-third (including the number of seats reserved for women belonging to the Scheduled

Castes and the Scheduled Tribes) of the total number of seats to be filled by direct election in every Municipality to be reserved for women and such seats to be allotted by rotation to different constituencies in a Municipality. [Article 243T(3)]

(xiv) Reservation of offices of Chairpersons in Municipality for the Scheduled Castes, the Scheduled Tribes and women in such manner as legislature of a State may by law provide. [Article 243T(4)]

2. LEGISLATIVE PROVISIONS

Legal Rights

To uphold the Constitutional mandate, the State has enacted various legislative measures intended to ensure equal rights, to counter social discrimination and various forms of violence and atrocities and to provide support services especially to working women.

Although women may be victims of any of the crimes such as 'murder', 'robbery', 'cheating', etc., the crimes, which are directed specifically against women, are characterized as 'Crime Against Women'. These are broadly classified under two categories.

1. The Crimes Identified Under the Indian Penal Code (IPC)

(i) Rape (Section 376 IPC).

(ii) Kidnapping and Abduction for different purposes (Section 376-373).

(iii) Homicide for Dowry, Deaths or their attempts (Sections 302/304-B IPC).

(iv) Torture, both mental and physical (Section 498 A IPC).

(v) Molestation (Section 354 IPC).

(vi) Sexual Harassment (Section 509 IPC).

(vii) Importation of girls (up to 21 years of age) (Section 366 B).

2. **The Crimes Identified Under the Special Laws (SLL)**

Although all laws are not gender specific, the provisions of law affecting women significantly have been reviewed periodically and amendments carried out to keep pace with the emerging requirements. Some Acts which have special provisions to safeguard women and their interests are:

(i) The Employees State Insurance Act, 1948
(ii) The Plantation Labour Act, 1951
(iii) The Family Courts Act, 1954
(iv) The Special Marriage Act, 1954
(v) The Hindu Marriage Act, 1955
(vi) The Hindu Succession Act, 1986
(vii) Immoral Traffic (Prevention) Act, 1956
(viii) The Maternity Benefit Act, 1961 (Amended in 1995)
(ix) Dowry Prohibition Act, 1961
(x) The Medical Termination of Pregnancy Act, 1971
(xi) The Contract Labour (Regulation and Abolition) Act, 1976
(xii) The Equal Remuneration Act, 1976
(xiii) The Child Marriage Restraint (Amendment) Act, 1983
(xiv) The Criminal Law (Amendment) Act, 1983
(xv) The Factories (Amendment) Act, 1986
(xvi) Indecent Representation of Women (Prohibition) Act, 1986
(xvii) Commission of *Sati* (Prevention) Act, 1987.

3. SPECIAL INITIATIVES FOR WOMEN

(i) National Commission for Women

In January 1992, the government set-up this statutory

body with a specific mandate to study and monitor all matters relating to the constitutional and legal safeguards provide for women, review the existing legislation to suggest amendments wherever necessary, etc.

(ii) Reservation for Women in Local Self-Government

The 73rd Constitutional Amendment Acts passed in 1992 by Parliament ensure one-third of the total seats for women in all elected offices in local bodies whether in rural areas or in urban areas.

(iii) The National Plan of Action for Girls Child (1991-2000)

The Plan of Action is to ensure survival, protection and development of the girl child with the ultimate objective of building up a better future for the girl child.

(iv) National Policy for the Empowerment of Women, 2001

The Department of Women and Child Development in the Ministry of Human Resource Development has prepared a "National Policy for the Empowerment of Women" in the year 2001. The goal of this policy is to bring about the advancement, development and empowerment of women.

Indian Constitution like many modern constitutions was also, a "break with the past" and was framed with, "a need for fresh look". Centuries of deliberate and concerted effort to deface the society by creating caste consciousness, exploiting religious sentiments was attempted to be effected by "The People".

The people of India through the Constitution resolved to constitute the country into a secular democratic republic. Preamble of the Constitution, echoing sentiments of nation, harassed for centuries by foreign domination, "to secure to all its citizens justice social economic and political; liberty of thought, expression belief, faith and worship. Equality of status and opportunity and to promote among them all fraternity assuring dignity of the individual" was not a mere flourish of words but was an ideal set-up for practice and observance as a matter of law through constitutional mechanism.

Employment or appointment to an office in the State constituted a, new form of wealth on the date the Constitution was enforced, therefore, equal opportunity to all its citizens was constitutionally provided for without any discrimination on religion, race or caste, etc. But it would have been mere illusion if no provision was made to ensure similar opportunity to those citizens who remained backward either because of historically social reasons or economic poverty or poor quality of education or any other reason which could be determinative of backwardness.

The National Human Rights Commission (NHRC) was set up in 1993 as a statutory body to which individuals and interested parties can make complaints on human rights violations in the country. The NHRC has explicitly stated that women's right will be a part of its concerns. As yet the NHRC has taken up no specific issue of violation, though it has attempted to address single instances of State of violence on woman. It is yet to take a significant interest in woman's rights. Part of the problem arises out of the division seen between the National Commission for Women and the NHRC; although a member of the women's commission is represented on the NHRC, it is often assumed that the women's commission will deal primarily with women's right violations. The NHRC's ability to function as an autonomous body is yet to be established. Like the women's commission, its establishment has been criticized as a move on the State to appear accountable without providing these bodies with sufficient autonomy to push through decisions or recommendations that may appear contrary to State interests. The Law Commission, the

Minorities Commissions, the Commission for Scheduled Tribes and Scheduled Castes that have been set-up are broadly mandated to look at women's issued, barring the Law Commission which has participated actively in recommending gender just legal change, the remaining commissions have shown little concern for women's rights in their functioning.

The causes of gender inequality are complex, linked as they are to the intra-household decision-making process. However, the decisions are made, the intra-household allocation of resources is influenced by market signals and institutional norms that do not capture the full benefits to society of investing in women. Low levels of education and training, poor health and nutritional status, and limited access to resources depress women's equality of life and creates hurdle in economic efficiency and growth. Regional perspectives play a very important role in the realm of gender equality.

The principle of gender equality is enshrined in the Indian Constitution in its Preamble, Fundamental Rights, Fundamental Duties and Directive Principles. However, there still exists a very wide gap between the goals enunciated in the Constitution, Legislation, policies, plans, programmes and related mechanisms on the one hand and the situational related of the status of women in India on the other.

The causes of persistent disparity and inequality between men and women are only partially examined, explored and understood. In recent years, attention has focused on inequalities in the allocation of resources at the household level, as seen in the higher share of education, health and food expenditures boys receive in comparison to girls. The decision-making process within households is complex and is influenced by social and cultural norms, market opportunities and institutional factors. There is considerable proof that the intra-household allocation of resources according to household members is a key factor in determining the levels of schooling, health and nutrition. Regional factors also have contributed in gender equalities.

Once of the fundamental obstacles to promoting gender equality in development remains at the community level where attitudinal biases often prevent women from realizing their rights. The government has done little to take on-board these obstacles, apart from occasional irregular campaigns around single issues like dowry, girl child education, amniocentesis and so on. Police education campaigns are restricted to occasional posters and T.V. spots, but are not consistent or backed up by strong and clear action by the State. Their impact remains less than effective, particularly since there is little action taken against advertising or campaigns that are gender-discriminatory.

Gender based discrimination represents ugly face of the society. This issue is global with varying degree and very old really, it is a travesty of all canons of social justice and equity that women who constitute half of the world's population and account for two-thirds of world's working hours should hold just 1/10th of world's property and still remain victim of inequality and injustice. This paradoxical anomaly is, now being openly questioned and the underlying discriminative process is seriously challenged.

Gender based discrimination at the UN is monitored by CEDAW, i.e. "Contention of the Elimination of All Forms of Discrimination against Women" in this context in respect of Article 11 of the UN resolution states that—

Violence and Equality in Employment

Equality in employment can be seriously impaired when women are subjected to gender specific violence such as sexual harassment in the workplace.

States should include in their reposts information about

sexual harassment, and on measures to protect women from sexual harassment and other forms of violence of coercion in the workplace.

It is just and reasonable procedure prescribed to achieve the constitutional objectives of equality in result, of status and opportunity and dignity of person to integrate them in the mainstream of the national life, as per the arch of the Constitution, i.e. the Preamble, Articles 14, 15, 16, and 46 of the Constitution and all other related Articles of the Constitution consistent with the efficiency of administration envisaged under Article 335 of the Constitution.

Thus, we see that our constitutional framer envisaged gender equality and women empowerment. It is sad and heartening that much needs to be done at the grass-root level.

❐

5

Gender Equality

Dignity Without Equality Not Possible

The aim of any civilized society should be to secure dignity to every individual. There cannot be dignity without equality of status and opportunity. The absence of equal opportunities in any walk of social life, a denial of equal status and equal participation in the affairs of the society and, therefore, of its equal membership. The dignity of the individual is dented and direct proportion to his deprivation of the equal access to social means. The democratic foundations are missing when equal opportunity to grow, govern, and give one's best to the society is denied to sizable section of the society. The deprivation of the opportunities may be direct or indirect as when the wherewithals to avail of them are denied. Nevertheless, the consequences are as potent.

Equal Amount of Work and Payment

It is really surprising to think that if women paid each other to do their housework, GNP would nearly double. It is not of course that wish to value all work and caring in monetary terms, but it does seem that because such work is undervalued, women's abilities and contribution throughout society and throughout the world also tend to be undervalued. It is interesting that in parts opportunities, not only amongst individuals but also among groups of people residing in different areas or nagged in different vocations, and Article 46 which enjoins upon the State to promote with special care the educational and economic interests of the weaker sections of the people, and to protect them from social injustice and all forms of exploitations, and Article 335 which requires the State to take into consideration the claim of Scheduled Castes and Scheduled Tribes in making the appointments to services and posts under the Union States, would have, all probably remained on paper.

Equality of Opportunities in Service

Thus, Article 16(1) and (4) operate in same field. Both are directed towards achieving equality of opportunity in services under the State. One is broader in sweep and expensive in reach. Other is limited in approach and narrow in applicability. Former applies to 'all' citizens whereas latter is available to 'any' class of backward citizens. Use of words 'all' in Article 16(1) is a fundamental right of a citizen whereas Article 16(4) is an obligation of the State. The former is enforceable in a court of law, whereas the latter is "not constitutional compulsion" but an exception "a *proviso* (Khanna, J., in The New Egalitarianism) or, "emphatic way of putting the extent to which equality of opportunity could be carried (Mathew, J., in *The New Egalitarianism*). "Presumed to exhaust all exception in favour of backward class," or "expressly designed as benign discrimination decocted to lifting of backward classes" but if Article 16(1) is the "positive aspect of equality of opportunity", Article 16(4) is a complete code for reservation for backward class of citizens as it not only provides for exercise of power but also lays down the circumstances, in which the power can be exercised, and the purpose and extent of its exercise. One is mandatory and operates automatically whereas the other comes into play on identification of backward class of citizens and their inadequate representation.

Equality, the Right of Child

Equality, the right of the child is the concern of the society so that fallen woman surpass trafficking of her person from exploitation; contribute to bring up her children, live a life with dignity, and not continue in the foul social environment. Equally the children have the right to equality of opportunity, dignity and care, protection and rehabilitation by the society with both hands open to bring them into the mainstream of social stratum by giving the same opportunities consideration with diverse perspectives, to decide the problems in the light of constitutional and human rights and direction given to the executive to effectuate them on administrative side effectively so that those rights become real and meaningful to them.

Question of Gender Equality

The question of gender equality is very old and burning problem. Twenty years ago in Mexico the First World Conference on Women inspired a movement that has helped to reduce gender inequality worldwide. Illiteracy among women is declining, maternal mortality and total fertility rates are beginning to fall, and more women are participating in the labour force than even before. However, much remains to be done. Persistent inequality between women and men constrains a society's productivity and, ultimately, slows its rate of economic growth. Although this problem has been generally recognized, evidence on the need for corrective action is more compelling today than ever.

Reservation Means to Achieve Equality

Reservation is not an end in itself. It is a means to

achieve equality. The policy of reservation adopted to achieve that end must, therefore, be consistent with the objective in view. Reservation must not outlast its constitutional object, and must not allow a vested interest to develop and perpetuate itself. There will be no need for reservation or preferential treatment once equality is achieved. Achievement and preservation of equality for all classes of people, irrespective of their birth, creed, faith or language is one of the noble ends to which the Constitution is dedicated. Every reservation founded on benign discrimination, and justifiably adopted to achieve the Constitution mandate of equality, limited in duration, conditional in application and specific in object. Reservation must contain within itself the seeds of its termination. Any attempt to perpetuate reservation and upset the constitutional mandate of equality is destructive of liberty and fraternity and all the basic values enshrined in the Constitution. A balance has to be maintained between the competing values and the rival claims and interests so as so achieve equality and freedom for all.

Right Against Exploitation

Traffic in human beings and beggar and other similar forms of forced labour are prohibited and any contravention of this provision shall be an offence punishable in accordance with law.

Nothing in this Article shall prevent the State from imposing compulsory service for public purpose, and in imposing such service the State shall not make any discrimination on grounds only of religion, race, caste or class or any of them.

Sexual Harassment and Violation of Fundamental Rights

Each such incident of sexual harassment results in the violation of the fundamental right of 'Gender Equality and the Right to Life and Liberty. It is a clear violation of the right under Article 14, 15 and 21 of the Constitution.

Every Indian under Article 13(I)g has a fundamental right to practice any profession or to carry out any occupation, trade or business. If women because of their fairer sex get hostile working environment which is unsafe for their security, dignity and liberty they are forced to underperform.

Such violation attracts the remedy under Act 32 of the constitution for this very reason.

To carry and their profession, trade or occupation a women requires a safe working environment.

Right to life under Act 21 in our Indian constitution means life to live with dignity. The primary responsibility for ensuring such safety and dignity lies with our Indian legislation and execution. Whenever violation occurs it becomes the prime duty of our legislature to make such laws which safeguard the safety of women. Justice delayed is Justice denied so there should be effective red venal of the grievances of the women for the protection of their rights.

GENDER TIMES

The same passions in man and woman nonetheless differ in tempo; hence man and woman do not case misunderstanding cause for another.

—Friedrich Nietzsche

During one cold November week in 1795, Martha Bullard of Hallowell, Maine, listed among her household chores: brewing beer, nursing a sick cow and scouring 35 skeins of wool in preparation for weaving. "A woman's work is never done, as the song says," she wrote in her diary that week. "And happy she whose strength holds out to the end of the days."

In addition to age-stratification, the only other cultural universal by which social roles are allocated is on the basis of gender. Numerous are the temporal strategies for keeping women in their place. The female role has, across cultures and history, been generally characterized by its greater temporal demamds, greater age discriminations, and by having to perform a greater number of rituals of temporal deference (e.g. being typically being younger than one's spouse).

		All Wives	**All Husbands**	**Wives Working Full Time With Children Under 18**	**Husbands With Children and Working Wives**
Percent of Adults Who Say the Wife	does the most cooking	78%	69%	64%	56%
	does the most house cleaning	74%	70%	66%	58%
	does the most food shoping	69%	61%	62%	53%
	does the most childcare	68%	41%	56%	28%
	does the most bill paying	57%	45%	61%	42%
	does the most household repairs	17%	8%	22%	12%
Percent of Adults	does MORE than his	11%	46%	16%	51%

Who Say the Wife	or her fair share of chores				
	does his or her fair share of chores	61%	48%	40%	47%
	does LESS than his or her fair share of chores	26%	27%	3%	42% 3%
Percent of Adults Who Say	they do not get enough time to them- selves	47%	37%	84%	49%
	the men are willing to let women get ahead, but only if women still do all the house work at home	57%	39%	60%	38%
	the women's movement has made things harder for men at home	53%	55%	59%	65%

THE DOUBLE STANDARD OF AGING

Why are men allowed to age without penalty while women must look young and lie about their age or risk disqualification from the sexual and marriage markets? Throughout the animal kingdom, the female is the longer-lived sex and yet for years the U.S. Department of Labour labelled women as 'old' at age 35 and males 'old' at 45.

Education and Economic Development

According to 1992-93 figures, only 9.2 per cent of the households in India were female-headed. However, approximately 35 per cent of the households below the poverty line were found to be female-headed.

Education

Though it is gradually rising, the female literacy rate in India is lower than the male literacy rate. Compared to boys, far fewer girls are enrolled in the schools, and many of them dropout. According to the National Sample Survey Data of 1997, only the States of Kerala and Mizoram have approached universal female literacy rates. According to majority of the scholars, the major factor behind the improved social and economic status of women in Kerala is literacy.

Under Non-Formal Education programme (NFE), about 40 per cent of the centers in States and 10 per cent of the centres in UTs are exclusively reserved for females. As of 2000, about 0.3 million NFE centres were catering to about 7.42 million children, out of which about 0.12 million were exclusively for girls. In urban India, girls are nearly at par with the boys in terms of education. However, in rural India, girls continue to be less educated than the boys.

According to a 1998 report by U.S. Department of Commerce, the chief barrier to female education in India are inadequate school facilities (such as sanitary facilities), shortage of female teachers and gender bias in curriculum (majority of the female characters being depicted as weak and helpless).

Workforce Participation

Contrary to the common perception, a large per cent of women in India work. The national data collection agencies accept the fact that there is a serious under-estimation of women's contribution as workers. However, there are far fewer women in the paid workforce than there are men. In urban India, women have impressive number in the workforce. As an example at software industry 30 per cent of the workforce is female. They are at par with their male counterparts in terms of wages, position at the workplace.

In rural India, agriculture and allied industrial sectors employ as much as 89.5 per cent of the total female labour. In overall farm production, women's average contribution is estimated at 55 per cent to 66 per cent of the total labour. According to a 1991 World Bank report, women accounted for 94 per cent of total employment in dairy production in India. Women constitute 51 per cent of the total employed in forest-based small-scale enterprises.

One of the most famous female business success stories is the Shri Mahila Griha Udyog Lijjat Papad. In 2006, Kiran Mazumdar-Shaw, who started Biocon one of India's first biotech companies, was rated India's richest woman. Lalita Gupte and Kalpana Morparia (both were the only businesswomen in India who made the list of the Forbes World's Most Powerful Women), run India's second-largest bank, ICICI Bank.

Land and Property Rights

In most Indian families, women do not own any property in their own names, and do not get a share of parental property. Due to weak enforcement of laws protecting them, women continue to have little access to land property. In fact, some of the laws discriminate against women, when it comes to land and property rights.

The Hindu personal laws of mid-1956s (applied to Hindus, Buddhists, Sikhs and Jains) gave women rights to inheritance. However, the sons had an independent share in the ancestral property, while the daughter's shares were based on the share received by their father. Hence, a father could effectively disinherit a daughter by renouncing his share of the ancestral property, but the son will continue to have a share in his own right. Additionally, married daughters, even those facing marital harassment, had no residential rights in the ancestral home. After amendment to Hindu laws in 2005, now women in ancestral home have been provided the same status as that of men.

In 1986, the Supreme Court of India ruled that Shah Bano, an old divorced Muslim woman was eligible for maintenance money. However, the decision was vociferously opposed by fundamentalist Muslim leaders, who alleged that the Court was interfering in their personal law. The Union Government subsequently passed the Muslim Women's (Protection of Rights Upon Divorce) Act.

Similarly, the Christian women have struggled over years for equal rights of divorce and succession. In 1994, all the churches, jointly with women's organizations, drew up a draft law called the Christian Marriage and Matrimonial Causes Bill. However, the government has still not amended the relevant laws.

Crimes Against Women

Police records show high incidence of crimes against women in India. The National Crime Records Bureau data shows an increase of 4.8% more crime against women during 2010 preceding the year 2009. Earlier many cases were not registered with the police due to the social stigma attached to rape molestation cases. Official statistics show that there has been a dramatic increase in the number of reported crimes against women.

Sexual Harassment

Half of the total number of crimes against women reported in 1990 related to molestation and harassment at the workplace. Eve teasing is a euphemism used for sexual harassment or molestation of women by men. Many activists blame the rising incidents of sexual harassment against women on the influence of 'Western Culture'. In 1987, The Indecent Representation of Women (Prohibition) Act was passed to prohibit indecent representation of women through advertisements or in publications, writings, paintings, figures or in any other manner.

In 1997, in a landmark judgement, the Supreme Court of India took a strong stand against sexual harassment of women in the workplace. The Court also laid down detailed guidelines for prevention and redressal of grievances. The National Commission for Women subsequently elaborated these guidelines into a code of conduct for employers.

Dowry

In 1961, the Government of India passed the Dowry Prohibition Act, making the dowry demands in wedding arrangement illegal. However, many cases of dowry-related domestic violence, suicides and murders have been reported. In the 1980s, numerous such cases were reported.

In 1985, the Dowry Prohibition (maintenance of lists of presents to the bride and bridegroom) rules were framed. According to these rules, a signed list of presents given at the time of the marriage to the bride and the bridegroom should be maintained. The list should contain a brief description of each present, its approximate value, the name of whoever has given the present and his/her relationship to the person. However, such rules are hardly enforced.

A 1997 report claimed that at least 5,000 women die each year because of dowry deaths, and at least a dozen die each day in 'kitchen fires' thought to be intentional. The term for this is 'bride burning' and is criticized within India itself. Amongst the urban educated, such dowry abuse has reduced considerably.

Child Marriage

Child marriage has been traditionally in India and continues to this day. Historically, young girls would live with their parents until they reached puberty. In the past, the child widows were condemned to a life of great agony, shaving heads, living in isolation and shunned by the society. Although child marriage was outlawed in 1860, it is still a common practice.

According to UNICEF's 'State of the World's Children-2009' report, 47 per cent of India's women aged 20-24 were married before the legal age of 18, with 56 per cent in rural areas. The report also showed that 40 per cent of the world's child marriages occur in India.

Female Infanticides and Sex Selective Abortions

India has a highly masculine sex ratio, the chief reason being that many women die before reaching adulthood. Tribal societies in India have a less masculine sex ratio that all other caste groups. This, in spite of the fact that tribal communities have far lower levels of income, literacy and health facilities. It can be attributed to female infanticides and sex-selective abortions.

All medical tests that can be used to determine the sex of the child have been banned in India, due to incidents of these tests being used to get rid of unwanted female children before birth. Female infanticide (killing of girl infants) is still prevalent in some rural areas. The abuse of the dowry tradition has been one of the main reasons for sex-selective abortions and female infanticides in India.

Domestic Violence

The incidents of domestic violence are higher among the lower socio-economic classes (SECs). The Protection of Women from Domestic Violence Act, 2005 came into force on October 26, 2006.

Trafficking

The Immoral Traffic (Prevention) Act was passed in 1956. However, many cases of trafficking of young girls and women have been reported. These women are either forced into prostitution, domestic work or child labour.

6

Woman and Law

(Laws Related to Violence Against Women)

WOMEN'S RIGHTS RELATED TO POLICE

Rights During Interrogation

1. You cannot be taken to the police station or anywhere else for interrogation.
2. You can be questioned only at your residence and in presence of your family members.
3. You can consult with your lawyer when you are being interrogated whether you are arrested or not.
4. You cannot be forced to make confession before the police or before the Magistrate.

Rights at Time of Arrest

5. You must be told why you are arrested, of your right to bail and of your right to a lawyer of your choice.
6. No use of handcuffs at the time of your arrest without a Judge's Permission.
7. You can demand that you be produced before the Magistrate within 24 hours of your arrest.
8. A female constable must be present when you are arrested.

9. You can take along your relative or friend to the police station.
10. The police arresting you must wear clear and visible nametag on uniform.
11. Memo of Arrest to be made, with date and time of arrest and signed by a family member/respectable neighbour.
12. The police must inform any person interested in your welfare, if such person lives outside the area, your arrest and the location of the place at which you are kept while under arrest.
13. An Accurate List of thing seized from you must be prepared and you are entitled to copy immediately.

Rights in the Police Station

14. You have the right to demand that you should be placed in a Female Lockup.
15. You have the right to ask the Magistrate for your medical examination if you are beaten, abused or tortured by the police.

Rights of Medical Examination

16. Request immediate medical examination on arrest. The medical examiner must record all injuries on a written form. Only sign an accurately filled form.
17. Ask for a copy of this.
18. Ask the Magistrate to send you to hospital before the police custody is granted.
19. A medical examination every 48 hours while in custody.
20. If you are under 18 years of age and your age is recorded wrongly, if there is no documentary proof of your age, insist on medical examination to determine your age.
21. Make an application for medical treatment in case of unstable health conditions.

Rights at the Time of Search

22. Search by a female officer only.
23. Two independent witnesses should always be present when you/your premises are searched.
24. Call two witnesses to witness the search.

Production in Court

25. You can demand a chair from the court to sit during trial.
26. You have the right to get legible copies of all document of accusation field against you in the court.
27. You can demand food and other basis amenities during your custody in the court.
28. You have to be produced before a Magistrate within twenty-four hours of arrest. If you are not produced within 24 hour complain to the Magistrate.
29. You cannot remand to custody in your absence.

Torture is Illegal

1. Torture is illegal. No solitary confinement, punitive cells, hard labour, change in the diet or transfers without permission of judge.
2. If a confession has been taken after torture, inform the judge immediately and retract it complaint to court about torture/beating and show any injuries. State must pay compensation for illegal arrest/torture.

Children and Juveniles

1. In case of persons under 18 years of age, age to be verified by documents or medical examination.
2. No remand to jail or police lockup. Must send to Juvenile Homes.
3. All investigations to complete within 4 months of complaints/F.I.R. and an enquiry before the Juvenile Justice Board.

Legal Advice

1. If poor, you have a right to demand a competent counsel at State expenses from the court.
2. If your lawyer is not competent, you have the right to change your lawyer.
3. You have a right to interviews, visits, and confidential communications with your lawyer.

Bail

1. Keep the following ready for production on grant of bail:
   Proofs of identity like salary slips, rent receipts ration cards, bank pass books, etc.
   Sureties with above documents.
2. If you are refused bail you have a right to get bail if:
   The charge-sheet is not filled within 60 days of arrest where your offence is punishable with imprisonment of less than 10 years.
   The charge-sheet is not filed within 90 days of arrest where your offence is punishable with imprisonment of more than 10 years.
3. If your bail is set too high, apply for reduction.

First Information Report (FIR)

1. You can demand that your FIR be registered.
2. You can take along any friend or relative at the time of filing FIR.
3. You must read the FIR or have some one else read it you, before you sign it.
4. You have a right to receive a free copy of the FIR.
5. You can approach to senior police officers or your area Magistrate, if the police is not registering your FIR.

Prison Custody

1. Persons below the age of 18 must be sent to an observation home only.

2. You have the right to write and receive letters.
3. You have the right to meet with your family and friends.
4. You can receive books, newspapers and other publications.
5. You may have a journalist to interview you.
6. You have to get reasonable wages for your labour while in prison.
7. You have a right to decent food, soap, clothing, bedding, etc.
8. You cannot be transferred to prisons in far away places.

HIV+ Or Terminal Illness

1. You may be entitled to premature release.

Parole

1. According to the rules, you may leave prison for certain periods for specific reasons.

Rape

1. Rape is an offence not against the individual but like all the crimes in the Indian Penal Code (IPC), it is a crime against the State.
2. Once the incident occurs, it has to be reported immediately without any delay to the police station of jurisdiction. As far as possible the complaint must be given in writing containing all relevant facts in order to avoid manipulation. Then the police will investigate the matter and file charge-sheet.
3. The information, i.e. the person filing the complaint is entitled to a copy of the First Information Report (FIR).
4. The victim must undergo medical examination conducted by a female medical officer.
5. The trial is conducted in a Court of Sessions.

6. Like all criminal matters, the victim cannot have an independent lawyer, unless she makes an application for appointing a Special Prosecutor. Any advocate with 10 years of practice can be appointed as a Special Public Prosecutor.

❒

7

Eve Teasing – The Concept

The term 'eve teasing' is used to refer to sexual harassment of women in public place such as the streets, public transportation, parks, beaches, and cinema-halls, etc. This type of a public harassment by a lone man or gang of men includes such as verbal assaults like as making passes or unwelcome sexual jokes; non-verbal assaults such as showing obscene gestures, winking, whistling, and staring and physical assaults such as pinching, fondling and rubbing against women in public places. In addition, several instances of eve teasing have been followed by more violent assaults such as rape and murder. Eve teasing is euphemistic expressions that lives in post-colonial India and refers largely to sexual harassment of women to provoke men into sexual titillation. This popular perception of sexual harassment poses the phenomena as a joke where women both a tease object and suffers simultaneously teasing ranges in severity from sexually coloured remarks to outright groping. It is the same story everyday.

Eve teasing may sound obscene but harmless in its behaviour but this act of molesting women has sometimes resulted in rape and even death of the victim. In one such horrific instance in Bihar, few young guys eve teased a 18 years old college girl on her way home; she was outraged and yelled at the guys. Next day the girl was kidnapped, raped and beaten by the same men until she was dead.

What right did these men have to violate the integrity of a woman for no fault of hers and why is eve teasing supposed to be a thing we are supposed to live with.

What is Eve Teasing?

It means a word used in India, Bangladesh and Pakistan for sexual harassment or molestation of women by men. Considered a growing problem throughout the sub-continent, eve teasing ranges in severity from sexually suggestive remarks to outright groping.

It is a serious evil maligning the society and plays havoc in the name of violence committed against women. Though the words are used in a frivolous manner many times and guys seem to take it like a sports, many girls are affected by it. They lose their confidence; feel ashamed of their bodies and some take action like suicide too.

It is the beginning of sexual discrimination and harassment and mild form of violence against women on street.

It is the beginning of identifying women as an object of lust and to molest them for rustication of sexual desires.

I happened to be to attend a seminar where eminent personalities participate. One of them was the District Judge and his very version was that men are like oxen free to move anywhere in the society while it is for the girls themselves to see to it that they are protected and do not face eve teasing.

Thus, the very being of woman as a human being is put at stake and she is to be only treated in the name of femininity.

Her very existence is marred by her destiny of being born a girl.

Many a times, it so happens that intelligent girls are not sent to good co-ed schools because of the underlying fear in their parents that the status of the girls could be affected by violence targeted at her.

Eve Teasing in India—Some Facts and Figures

I goggled eve teasing and found many hits. Some thought-provoking and shocking facts and figures about eve teasing in India are as follows:

1. The expression eve teasing is Indian in origin. You won't find it in most of the dictionaries. Native speakers of English do not use it.
2. Students show that 32 per cent of the eve teasers are students, 35 per cent are anti-socials while the remaining 33 per cent are middle-aged men.
3. The number of registered case of sexual crimes against women in India increases from 67,072 in 1988 to 84,000 in 1993. In 1995 alone, more than 25,000 cases of molestation and 12,000 cases of rape were reported in the capital city of New Delhi. It is estimated that well over 80 per cent of the sexual crimes go unreported. For example, 7643 of the 50,000 estimated instance of violence against women were reported to the police even in Kerala, a south Indian State with the highest women's literacy rate.
4. An increasingly large number of college going women taking public transportation in Delhi have resorted to carrying pins, pen knives and even daggers as a deterrent. Other have taken self-defense classes.
5. A recent survey has revealed that approximately 90% of college women in New Delhi have experienced sexual harassment in some form or another.
6. Nighty-eight per cent of the women have stated that sexual harassment on roads has affected their personal or academic development in one way or the other.

These facts may appear untrue and horrifying but they clearly show the plight of women in India. The condition is deteriorating everyday. It is high time, therefore, that we include eve teasing as a tort under a new head of liability and curb this heinous practice.

Eve Teasing—The Psychology Behind

Many psychologists believe that sex, love or fun is not the only motive that men indulge in his behaviour. Eve teasing is closely related to the patriarchal mindset of the Indian male. Men are raised to believe that they are more powerful physically and emotionally than women. They feel that they are doing nothing wrong in just having some fun. Women on the other hand are made to feel vulnerable and the weaker sex.

Teacher of psychology and social scientists believe eve teasing to be a result of the frustration suffered by a majority of youth. Disappointed by the unbecoming attitude of teachers and indifferent parents, they yearn for an outlet to vent their aggression and depression. Besides, many who do not inherit good values tend to indulge in acts of sexual harassment.

At the risk of cover simplifying a complex phenomenon, it would not be imprudent to say that in our country, the construct of masculinity is usually equated with patriarchy. In other words, masculinity is experienced not so much as a set of emotional or behavioural characteristics unique to the male gender, but more in terms of hierarchical domination over the feminine gender; so that the most feminine man gets a socially dominant position over his female counterpart.

Gender segregation from childhood, lopsided parental relationships as well as the representation of man-woman relationship in literature and popular cinema, all serve to reinforce the patriarchal model of masculinity in the mind of the growing male child.

The vocal emergence of feminism has also pushed the contemporary male a little of the backfoot, not only the women are threading to encroach on her male dominion, but also he does not have any idea about how he can counter encroach on hers. Organized sport and cultural activates are examples of these, but require some talent and application. Whereas standing with a group of peers at a bus stop or in a cineplex, passing lewd remarks, gesticulation lasciviously and generally behaving obnoxiously requires mere number and when the hapless girl is in no position to defend herself despite visible evidence of distress, domination gets established.

Thus, we tried to understand the psychology of an average eve teaser when he indulges himself in the heinous practice.

All this study has been done only to establish the fact further strongly that it is now high time to include eve teasing as a separated tort so that this injustice and crime against the honour and dignity of the women can be stopped.

Eve Teasing and Tortious Liabilities

I am sure reading the previous pages must have forced you to think about the plight of the Indian women. Mere thinking would not do in the present era. We should come forward and take strong steps against this practice. Strong laws should be enforced to tackle this problem. Eve teasing should be taken as a grave offence against the dignity and honour of a woman.

We can start by making eve teasing as a separate head of a liability under the law of torts. When included in law as a civil wrong, it would certainly see a decline in the cases of eve teasing also the women will have a weapon in their hands to uphold their dignity. They will feel more empowered and independent.

Eve Teasing—A Tort

Let us examine eve teasing under the light of the three

essential elements of torts. Torts can be conceptualized to include the following essential elements.

Tort is a civil wrong.

This civil wrong is other than a mere breach of contract or breach of this wrong is repressible by an action for unliquidated damages.

Eve teasing is a civil wrong. The eve teaser causes injury to the plaintiff which in turn affects her both physically and mentally. It is an unlawful infringement on the victim's privacy and person. She is tortured in the process. It also hampers her peace and happiness. In other words, it curtails her light to enjoy her life and be happy.

Eve teasing is neither a breach of contract nor a breach of a trust. It is an encroachment on a woman's right and her dignity.

Eve teasing is an unexpected incident. There is no question of a contract in it. Thus, its remedy is unliquidated damages which are to be decided by the courts according to the gravity of the injury caused. The courts can also provide a remedy in the forms of injunction and detention also. This could force the eve teasers to at least think thrice before they indulge in such torts and its basic guiding principal of *Ubi Jus Ubi Remedium*, i.e. where there is violation of legal right, there has to be some relief, compensation and remedy for the victim.

Eve Teasing as a Trespass of Person

Every person's is inviolate. Interference, however, slight with a person's elementary civil right to security of the person, and self-determination in relation to his own body, constitutes to trespass to the person.

Eve teasing is the worst form of trespass to person possible. It is done intentionally to hurt a woman physically, emotionally and spiritually. It is also done to wrongfully gain the attention of the woman. It violated the person's elementary civil right to security of a person. It is a grave civil wrong against women. It is more torturous for small girls and adolescents.

The application of force to the person of another without lawful justification amounts to the wrong of battery. Avoidable physical contact and advances, touching, patting, whistling, pinching physical assault and molestation by the eve teasers amounts to battery. An unwanted physical touch, an unwanted kiss all amount to battery and are actionable by the law.

The act of putting another person in reasonable fear or apprehension of an immediate battery by means of an act amounting an attempt or treat to commit a battery amounts to an actionable assault. An eve teaser also commits as assault when he commits the shameful act of eve teasing.

Thus, we can say that eve teasing amounts to trespass to person as it constitutes both battery and assault.

Compensation and Remedies

Eve teasing is a civil wrong. It is an unlawful infringement of the victim's legal rights. So according to the principal of *Ubi Jus Ubi Remedia*, there should be a remedy for the victim in the cases of eve teasing.

This part is very important for many reasons.

Firstly, it gives relief to the victim's as she can recover the loss cause to her.

Secondly, it gives the victim immense satisfaction to see the eve teaser punished and admonished. She develops a sense of satisfaction, happiness and regains her confidence and self-esteem.

Thirdly, it gives a strict warning to the eve teasers so that they do not indulge in this heinous practice. It, thus, strongly condemns the practice of eve teasing.

The Remedies can be in the following forms:

Public Humiliation

The eve teasers should be humiliated publically so as to make them aware and feel guilty of the shameful practice that they indulged in. People should socially boycott them as to make them realize their mistake. Their names should be published in the newspapers describing their shameful act in detail so as to make them feel guilty and realize their mistakes.

Monetary Compensation

Damages should be awarded to the victim in terms of money. It should be big money. It will recover the loss that she must have suffered and also will discourage men from involving in eve teasing.

Injunction

The court can also ask the eve teasers to strictly abstain from indulging in eve teasing in case of repeated acts of similar kind.

Detention

The court could also arrest a person for eve teasing under Article 57, CPC. This would further discourage people from eve teasing.

MOLESTATION/EVETEASING AT: PREVENTIVE STEPS A SAFE GUARD AGAINST EVE TEASING

Home

Many young girls have faced situations where an uncle, brother is overtly friendly. They are always hugging, trying to touch and feel you up under the guise of fatherly/ brotherly love or trying to tickle you, etc. Due to family relations, even the girls feel awkward to say much. Sometimes girls are not even sure if the accidental pressing/ touching was indeed accidental or intentional.

In this case, trust your instincts and avoid their company as much as possible. If he gets out of hand, report to your mother or some female relative. Know one thing, an accidental touch/press can happen once or twice maybe, will not happen regularly. So if happens more twice—know that it is intentional.

School

Many girls face problems with guys in school. The teenage boys with their hormonal imbalance is a big problem. They sometimes try to touch accidentally or bump into a girl and try to touch her bosom/bottom. Specially, girls who are attractive or have 'developed more' face this issue. Tolerate a little but if they are repeating it—report to a female teacher or the principal.

College

Due to the 'open' atmosphere in colleges and the revealing clothes of girls, many guys think that women crave attention and are of 'loose' character. So avoid too revealing clothes and be careful how your image in college is. Try to dress like other girls and play safe.

Be careful specially in the loo. Today phone cameras are rampant and are often misused and planted in loo, swimming pools, etc.

Office

Many times, men in power try to misuse their position and try to abuse girls.

Girls: This is complicated as men are more mature and do eve teasing in a disguise—

1. It is better to avoid such men.
2. Do not wear revealing clothes to office. Too tight tops/skirts/pants are not a good idea.
3. Try to be careful when you bend down in front of others. Be careful in adjusting your clothes in the office.

4. If men go over the limit (by making any sexual comments/jokes/staring openly), tell them frankly on their face.
5. Complain to the Boss/HR as a last resort (no one likes a cry baby).

Though this has been written from my experience, hope this will help women all over India.

What are Laws Available Against This Crime?

Five legal remedies available in the form of compensation to the plaintiff—

Existing Provisions

Sections 294 and 509 of the Indian Penal Code. A Bill on the same subject was earlier introduced and passed by the Rajya Sabha in 1988.

While pending before the Lok Sabha, due to dissolution of the Lok Sabha, the Bill lapsed.

Proposed Amendments by Government

A proposal for the enactment of the Delhi Prohibition of Eve Teasing Bill, 1992 received from the Ministry of Home Affairs (1992). The proposal referred to the Commission in 1992 contained the Delhi Eve Teasing Bill of 1984 which has been passed by the Delhi Metropolitan Council for adoption by Parliament.

Suggested Amendments by NCW

1. The short title and the enacting formula have to be suitably amended as the proposed Bill is being brought forward in 1993.
2. In view of the nature of the offence contemplated in the proposed Bill, the definition of 'man' as suggested in Clause 2 (b) of the proposed legislation may be omitted.

3. Clause 3 of the proposed legislation of 'Eve Teasing' appears to be only an amalgam of provisions of Sections 294 and 509 of the IPC.
4. The new legislation does not make any improvement but on the contrary appears to have diluted the punishment for the offence (vide Clause 4 of the Bill).

General Suggestions and Remarks

The lapsed Bill of 1988 was better drafted than the Delhi Prohibition of Eve Teasing Bill of 1984. Some of the voluntary organizations suggested that the expression 'Eve Teasing' should be replaced by a more appropriate expression suitable for the Indian context.

Eve Teasing in Bihar

1. **Now a medical student arrested on molestation charge in Patna**

The youth involved in the case is Manish Kumar who is incidentally an MBBS final year student of the Medical College. According to police, two girls were on way to their residence at Machuatoli after attending their IIT-JEE coaching class at Khazanchi road at around 6 p.m. on Wednesday. As they were walking a youth riding a motorcycle first passed lewd comments on them. After that he caught the hand of one of the girls. The official Pirbahore police station quoting the written complaint lodged by the girls, said that both the girls raised an alarm drawing the attention of the local residents. Upon this some students of the coaching institute reached the spot and even thrashed Manish. On getting information,the SHO of Pirbahore Police Station, Asrar Ahmad, reached the spot and arrested Manish. The girls in their complaints alleged that Manish was stalking them for at least the past 25 days. They further mentioned that Manish used to follow them even when they went for marking. However, Manish denied the charge and said that he had been falsely implicated in the case by the two girls. He said he was staying at the NMCH hostel and had come to PMCH to meet one of his friends.

2. Bihar Okays creation of 40 women police stations

The government will set-up one women police station in each police district. The government had also approved the creation of 643 posts, including 21 inspectors, 121 sub-inspectors, 101 assistant sub-inspectors, 80 havaldars and 324 constables for the women police station. Women police stations would be exclusive for women.

According to latest official statistics, a total of 6,790 cases of crime and atrocities on women have been registered in Bihar this year. Of them, 795 cases are of rap, 2,552 of kidnapping, 104 of eve teasing, 1,307 of dowry death and 2,032 of dowry torture.

3. Police seek action against ASI in eve teaching case

The Police would send a letter to the Bihar Military Police (BMP) commandant for initiating disciplinary action against an ASI, whose son Ravi Ranjan was involved in eve teaching at Income-Tax Roundabout on October 13. Two youth, who were boozing on the road near a liquor shop close to Income-Tax Roundabout, had tried to molest a BA part III student of Magadh Mahila College when she was waiting for her father there on October 13. When her father, who had reached there by that time, resisted their attempt, the inebriated youth also assaulted him in full public view. The police later released the sketches of the two youth and later received several calls identifying the youth as Pintu Singh and Ravi Ranjan residents of Polson at Digha and Birla Colony in Phulwarisharif respectively. Incidentally, Ranjan was earlier indentified as Ravi Prakash. Police would seek disciplinary action against the BMP ASI as he lied to the police that his son, who was allegedly involved in eve teaching, was studying at Delhi. Secondly, the ASI and his elder son Rakesh had appeared before the police with the document of the seized motorcycle with number plate of police. Rakesh had initially imprisonated his younger brother, Rajan Singh on Tuesday reached the Patna Civil Court to surrender in the court. Pintu was told in the court by some lawyers that his named did not figure in the FIR, so how can he surrender? He, however, escaped before the police, the police reached the court premises. The police team carried out raid at Rajan's house in Birla Colony. Though he was not present in the house, his wife was there and intensive raids were on to both the accused.

4. Gilrl helped by Naxal

A case of eve teasing came in light in Paraiya area of Bihar where Ranjit Kumar misbehaved with his student. Everyone in the area was afraid of the culprit; no one was brave enough to take action against him. The masses of the village took help of naxalite against it. The masses of the village took help of naxalite to punish the culprit and he was punished adequately.

5. One Arrested in Eve Teasing Case

Police in Patna on Thursday a week after some drunken men near the Income-Tax Roundabout on Bailey Road misbehaved with a college girl, arrested one Pintu Singh in the case after he was positively identified by some eyewitnesses through the composite pictures earlier released by the police. A sober, and rather scared, Singh told the police that he was drinking with some of his buddies but did not remember anything beyond that. One more person who was involved in the shameful incident is yet to be traced. Two men in a state of drunkenness teased a college student on one Thursday evening and made lewd remarks as she wanted for her father to come and pick her up. When the father showed up, the two men thrashed him but managed to flee before the police could reach the spot. The incident had sparked a riot like situation as people in the area blocked the road for hours demanding the arrest of the perpetuators.

Later the perpetuator was identified as one Pinto Signal by the eyewitnesses through the composite picture later released by the police. He accepted of misbehaving in a state of drunkenness. This sort of an incidence is a common day occurrence in most past of our country.

6. Eve Tease Dilemma for Cops

There is spurt in the incidents of eve teasing in our country and it is giving our police cops a sleepless night. The incidence of eve teasing molestation and sexual harassments are not only misconduct of social behaviour of men, but it is a crime. Thus the vigilant and watchful attitude of the police cops should be mandatory to curb it on streets and roads. A 45-year-old man was beaten up by the public this morning after he allegedly passed lewd comments on a girl and tried to pull her *dupatta*. The girl was standing in front of gate number 2 of the Patna Zoo when the man went close to her. She raised an alarm and the passers-by caught hold of him and beat him up before calling the police. He is in police custody at the moment. The man was behaving strangely and seemed mentally unstable.

7. One evening some residents at Patrakar Nagar bashed up a youth, whose friend was having a conversation with some girls. The girls were celebrating a friend's birthday when some boys approached them with birthday greetings. It was quite obvious that the boys and the girls knew each other. Some residents saw them talking and thought it to be an incident of eve teasing and attacked the boys. The boy who received maximum injuries had nothing to do with the incident. He was just accompanying his friends. Such incidents were unfortunate.
8. Another case of alleged eve teasing took a new twist today with principal of a women college claiming that a few students were targeting a

college staff by cooking up eve teasing allegations against him. A group of girls, all students of the physics department of the college, alleged that the laboratory in-charge had misbehaved with them on October 13. They claimed the man, identified as Manoj Kumar, had grabbed the hand of a student trying to pull her close. College principal however, denied the allegation.

9. "The college students are banned from using cell phones on campus. One of them was talking on her cell phone when the lab technician stopped her and snatched the phone. In the process, he touched her hand and the students turned the entire episode into an eve teasing incident. A written application regarding the same was given to me the next day. Today a group of girls stopped me and enquired what action I had taken in the matter", she added that a committee had already been formed to probe the complaint and the report will be sent to the Magadh University after *Chhath Puja*.

10. **Eve Teasing : US Tourist Assaulted in One of the States for Objecting**

An American tourist was assaulted when he tried to rescue his French friend from eve teasing at one of the tourist places in our country. The American suffered fracture in her left hand because of the assault. The police swiftly took action by arresting two of three suspects and filed charge-sheet within 16 hours of the incident requesting the court for speedy trial. The incident took place when US citizen Alex (26) and his travel companion from France, Curlyo (24), arrived in Rajgir from Bodh Gaya on Wednesday evening. They checked into Sadhu Line Hostel and went to move about Rajgir hills without any guide. Three locals, later identified as Sandesh Rajvanshi, Sanjay Rajvanshi and Balbir Paswan, chased them, passing snide comments on Curlyo. Alex toot offence to it and had an argument with the locals. All of three, who was carrying a stick, hit Alex several times. Alex has been shifted to his hostel after treatment at Rajgir Government Hospital.

11. Now women cops in Patna to look 'nice' and bait molesters!
12. In many state capitals, the police department has decided to nab the roving criminals with the help of women cops. The plan is to use women cops as lures and baits under the protection of their male counterparts. Patna Senior Superintendent of Police, Alok Kumar told the press that the constables at the Women's Helping, a wing of the city police that dealing with offence towards women, will be a part of the new campaign. It seems that such an attempt was made earlier but without sufficient protection from male colleagues in plain clothes. This will also allow the women cops to carry out the job even after dark, which is what the plan is.
13. According to the sources, the women constables concerned have been asked to dress 'nicely' to look attractive. With policemen in civil clothes nearby, the cops will move in and around crowded shopping complexes, malls and theatres. According to the police's 'observation, the really troublesome eve teasers sit in groups and move around in public place. The Women's Helpline, formed six month ago has done a good job and the cell received a lot of calls from women victims and action has been taken. The helping dealt with at least 500 cases in the past six months.
14. Selecting crowded places seems a good idea to begin with. But it is perhaps the relatively isolated areas with few pedestrians that deserve due

attention. These are areas where the molesters find victims easily and are also able to get away. A suggestion the police may check on sits favoured by chain snatchers, etc. or other attackers in the past to decide on the trend and then accordingly plan their movement.

15. By targeting 'groups' of boys, though the police department seems to have got its social profile right. The fact is that in a public place such groups are often identified by their look and behaviour quite easily. Women, unlike men, are especially sensitive to such potential trouble and tend to keep a distance. Of course, in the case of a woman cop, she would have to spot such groups and stay close if anything to attract attention. Rarely does a single and unaccompanied boy/man dare indulge in eve teasing and when they do the offence may remain confined to a remark or two. Also, the reason passers-by fail to react molestation attempts by large groups is quite obvious—the group is united and the passers-by taken a lot of time before they may taken united action which often depends on individual initiatives.

16. **Role of Police in Eve Teasing Cases**

Patna, Feb. 28 The city police are keeping their fingers crossed and desperately hoping that the *khaki*-clad man, who misbehaved with a schoolgirl in an autorickshaw last evening is not a cop.

17. The cops have launched a massive manhunt to nab the eve teaser. A team led by city Superintendent of Police, Shivdeep Lande has started tracking the man. The police are drawing up the sketch of the accused from the information provided by the girl. The uniform of guards of many security agencies is similar to the police or the Special Auxiliary Police, often leading to

confusion. The cops are now considering means to rectify the situation. Private agencies could be asked to change their uniforms, said a police officer.

18. On Sunday, the girl a student of Central School, Sheikhpura was on her way to a painting class in an autorickshaw. A man in a *khaki* uniform was also in the girl boarded. The uniformed co-passenger allegedly started misbehaving with her. The girl asked the autorickshaw driver to stop the vehicle near JD Women's College. But when she tried to get out, the man caught her hand. When the frightened girl raised an alarm, the autorickshaw driver sped away, with the man still in the vehicle.
19. The girl's family finally lodged an FIR with the Shastri Nagar Police Station later in the evening. Sanjay Kumar, the Station House Officer (SHO) of Shastri Nagar Police Station has been suspended by the SSP for not taking prompt action in the case. Her father is an Assistant Engineer with State Road Construction Department.
20. At present, the police were talking to the girl about the man so that the sketch can be prepared. With the sketch of the man with the police, the search can be narrowed down. All aspects of the accused are being considered. There are many agencies whose uniforms resemble that of the police we are truing to develop a system through which this problem can be solved.
21. This is not the first time that the police have been in an eveteasing case. On February 26, another girl had alleged that an officer of the quick mobile unit, near Patliputra Police Station had harassed her. The next day Sunil Singh, the policeman in question, revealed to his friend that Ramparvesh

Kumar had misbehaved with the girl, Singh was suspended for negligence of duty.

22. On Thursday, the girl, a resident of Jasidih in Jharkhand, was allegedly stripped by a group on the busy Exhibition Road in Patna.
23. How have you felt every time you ignored a stranger's eyes boring through your clothes? How often have you been witness to 'eve teasing'? How many times have you whistled, leached at, stalked or made lewd comments at a girl or a woman on the streets 'just for fun'? The Blank Noise Project ran an online poll asking respondents what specific acts they thought constituted sexual harassment.

A Reported Case: Headmaster Heed for Bad Intent

Patna: Jahanabad police on Friday arrested Subhas Ram headmaster of government middle school, Kinari, on charges of luring a school girl with bad intention.

Police swung into action, after the girl, a class VIII student of the middle school lodged an FIR with local police on Thursday accusing Ram of trying to lure her with a bad intention.

The headmaster, according to the FIR, asked the girl to accompany him to Rajgir and when she refused to budge, he hurried abuses at her and also threatened to concoct a false story regarding the girl's illicit relationship with a local boy.

The girl in her statement, also claimed that Ram had tried to act in a similar fashion on past and she is not the only victim of his intention. Some other school girls too had faced this situation in the past.

"Taking note of the statement given by the girl and her father Suresh Yadav, we arrested Ram and he was sent to judicial custody on Friday," a police official said.

Conclusion

Thus, we see that more and more we delve into this issue more alarming results would come out for eve teasing is just the way our men are made to behave towards women. Eve teasing is a social display of low esteem which is attached to women's status in society. Woman most of the time is a man show piece and until and unless the process of genderisation is such that woman come to accord their rightful position, in society, at home, in school, in relation. She will continue to be teased.

❐

8

Sexual Harassment at Workplace

No specific law regarding sexual harassment, Supreme Court has laid down guidelines in Vishaka'a case (AIR 1997 Supreme Court 3011).

Any unwelcome sexually determined behaviour—direct or implicit, viz.

1. Physical contact and advances
2. Demand or request for sexual favours
3. Sexually coloured remarks
4. Showing pornography
5. Any other unwelcomed physical, verbal or non-verbal conduct of sexual nature.

SUCH ACTS COMMITTED AMOUNTS TO SEXUAL HARASSMENT:

1. Where the victim has a reasonable apprehension
   - That such conduct is humiliating.
   - Constitutes health and safety problem.
2. When the victim has a reasonable ground to believe that her objections, acts would disadvantage, prejudice her in connection with work, recruitment, promotion, creates a hostile work atmosphere.
3. When non-consent objections to such acts entails adverse consequence.

DUTIES AND OBLIGATIONS AS PER JUDGMENT

- Duty to Prevent Commission of Acts of Sexual Harassment
  - (i) Identify the acts that constitute sexual harassment.
  - (ii) Prohibit acts of sexual harassment at workplace.
  - (iii) Penalize commission of acts of sexual harassment.
  - (iv) Abetment to be defined to include non-action of the official concerned.
  - (v) Notify, published and circulate – acts prohibited.
  - (vi) Provide congenial atmosphere – work – leisure and health – hygiene.
  - (vii) That no woman employee should have ground to believe that she is disadvantaged in connection with her work.
  - (viii) Provide optional transfer, if the victim feels necessary.
  - (ix) Incorporate sexual harassment in conduct rules.
  - (x) Incorporate the Industrial Standing Order.
  - (xi) Initiate criminal proceeding under IPC.
  - (xii) Ensure prevention to victimization and discrimination of victims and witnesses.
  - (xiii) Facilitated discussions in employee-employer meeting.
  - (xiv) Create awareness among women about sexual harassment.
- Duty to Provide Procedure for Resolution Complaint Mechanism Headed by Women.
- Duties of the committee:— Provide counselling, medical aid, legal aid, maintain confidentially and time-bound inquiry.

Hints for legislation—The hint for legislation to the Union Government that feasibility of a legislation safeguarding interest of women may be examined by incorporating such provisions as—

(1) No marriage between N.R.I. and an Indian women which has taken place in India, may be annulled by a foreign court.

(2) Provision may be made for adequate alimony to the wife in the property of the husband both in India and abroad.

(3) The decree granted by Indian Court may be made executable in foreign courts both on principles of comity and by entering into reciprocal agreements like Section 44A of the Civil Procedure Code, which makes a foreign decree executable as it would have been a decree passed by that court.

Our Journey to Vishaka—A Forum Against Sexual Harassment

Bhanwari Devi was a village-level social worker or a 'Saathin' of a development programmer run by the State Government of Rajasthan, fighting, against child and multiple marriages in villages. As part of this work, Bhanwari, with assistance from the local administration, tried to stop the marriage of Ramkaran Gujjar's infant daughter who was less than one year old. The marriage took place nevertheless, and Bhanwari earned the ire of Gujjar family. She was subjected to social boycott, and in September 1992 five men including Ramkaran Gujjar, gang raped Bhanwari in front of her husband, while they were working in their fields. The days that followed were filled with hostility and humiliation for Bhanwari and her husband. The only male doctor in the Primary Health Centre refused to examine Bhanwari and the doctor at Jaipur only confirmed her age without making any reference to rape in his medical report. At the police station, the women constables taunted Bhanwari throughout the night. It was past midnight when the policemen asked Bhanwari to leave her dress behind as evidence and return to her village. She was left with only her husband's bloodstained *dhoti* to wear. Their pleas to let them sleep in the police station at night were turned down. The trial court acquitted to accused, but Bhanwari was determined to fight further and get justice. She said that she had nothing to be ashamed of and that the men should be ashamed due to what they had done. Her fighting spirit inspired fellow saathins and women's groups countrywide. In the months that followed they launched a concerted campaign for justice for Bhanwari. On December 1993, the part of this campaign, the groups had filed a petition in the Supreme Court of India, under the name **Vishaka** asking the Court to give certain directions regarding the sexual harassment that women face at the workplace. The result is the Supreme Court Judgement, which came on 13th August 1997, and gave the **Vishaka** guidelines.

The lifestory of Bhanwari Devi brings to fore the blatant truth that indulging in self-pity and self-destruction can lead nowhere in life. She has acted as a torchbearer in common woman's search and defining of her identity. Protection of women against Sexual Harassment at Workplace Bill, 2010 would help in creating an enabling environment for women to work without any fear or any form of harassment that in turn would deter their withdrawal of employment from the labour market. This Bill however needs a careful discussion on its strengths and weaknesses as it has also left out the domestic workers from its purview.

Sexual Harassment and Violation of Fundamental Right

Each such incident results in violation of Fundamental Right of Gender Equality and the Right of Life and Liberty.

It is a clear violation of the rights under Articles 14, 15, 21 of the Constitution. One of the logical consequences of such an incident is also the violation of the Human Fundamental Right under Article 13(1)(g) to practice any profession or to carry any occupation trade or business. Such violation therefore attract the remedy under Article 32 of the Constitution for the enforcement of these Fundamental Rights of women. This clause action under Article 32 of the Constitution is for this reason.

Working Environment

Right to life means life with dignity. The primary responsibility for ensuring such safety and dignity through suitable legislation and the creation of mechanism for its enforcement is of legislates.

When however instance of sexual harassment resulting in violation of Fundamental Rights of women wake under Articles 17, 19 and 21 of the Constitution an effective red renal.

That some guideline should be land for the protection of these rights to file the legislative vacuum custodial rape on sub the persistent behaviour. Somebody come up with harassment. Sexual harassment: Instantly we acquired that's what it was.These activist in Farley.Susan Meyer& Karen saw vine went on to form working women's institute which along with the alliance against sexual coercion funded in 1976 by Freda Klein, Lynn we aril & Elizabeth Cohn stunts were among the pioneer organization to being sexual harassment to public attention in the late 1970's

Harassment Situations

Sexual harassment can occur in variety of circumstances often but a ways, the harasser is on a position of power a authority over the victim (due to difference in age), a social, political, educational or employment relationships. Forms of harassment relationship include:

(a) The harasse can be anyone such as a client, co-worker, a parent or a legal guardian, a teacher or professor, a student friend or a stranger.
(b) The victim does not have to be the person directly harassed but can anyone who finds the behaviour offensive and is affected by it.
(c) Adverse effects on the target are common.
(d) The victim and harasser can be any gender.
(e) The harasser does not have to be of the opposite sex.
(f) The harasser may be completely unaware that his or her behaviour is offensive or constitute sexual harassment or may be completely unaware that his or her action could be unlawful.
(g) Misunderstanding—It can result from a situation where one thinks he/she is making themselves clear but it not understood the way they intended. The misunderstanding can be either be reasonable a unreasonable. Sexual harassment is intimidation bullying or coercion or a sexual nature or the unwelcome or inappropriate promise of rewards in exchange for sexual favourer.

In some contexts or circumstances sexual harassment is illegal, it includes a range of behaviour from seemingly mild transgressors and annoyances to actual sexual abuse or sexual assort.

Sexual harassment is a form of illegal employment – discrimination in many countries and is a form of abuse (sexual and psychological) and bullying. For many organizations and businesses, preventing sexual harassment and defending employees from sexual harassment charges have become key goal of legal decision-making.

Early History of the Use of the Term

The term 'sexual harassment' was used in 1973 in a report to the then President and Chancellor of MIT, about various forms of gender issues (Sea satur's Rings 1974).

Rowe has stated that she believes she was not the first to use the term, since sexual harassment was being discussed in women's groups in Massachusetts in the early 1970s but that MIT may have been the first or one of the first large organizations to discuss the topic (in the MIT academic council) and to develop relevant policies and procedures.

In the book 'in our time, Memoir of a Revolution (1999) journalist Susan Brown Miller quotes the Cornell activist who in 1975 though they had coined the term sexual harassment. Eight of us were sitting in office — brainstorming about what we were going to write on posters for our speak out we were refining to it as sexual intimidation, sexual coercion. Sexual exploitation on the job none of names seemed quite right.

Shows a person any sexually explicit visual material, in the form of picture/cartoons/pin- ups/calendars/screen savers on computer/any offensive written material/ pornographic e-mail, etc.

Engages in any other unwelcome conduct of a sexual nature, which could be verbal, or even non-verbal, like staring to make the other person uncomfortable, making offensive gestures, kissing, sounds, etc.

It is sexual harassment if a supervisor requests sexual favours from a junior in return for promotion or other benefits or threatens to sack for non-cooperation. It is also sexual harassment for a boss to make intrusive inquiries into the private lives of employees, or persistently ask them. Its sexual harassment for a group of workers to joke and snigger amongst themselves about sexual conduct in an attempt to humiliate or embarrass another person.

Sexual harassment at workplace is generally classified into two distinct types. *'Quid pro quo'*, means seeking sexual favours or advances in exchange for work benefit and it occurs when consent to sexually explicit behaviours or speech is made a condition for employment or refusal to comply with a 'request' is met with retaliatory action such as dismissal, demotion, difficult work condition. 'Hostile working environment' is more pervasive form of sexual harassment involving work conditions or behaviours that make the work environment 'hostile' for the woman to be in. Certain sexist remarks, display of pornography or sexist/obscene graffiti, physical contact/bushing against female employees are some examples of hostile work environment, which are not made conditions for employment.

Unwelcome

UNWELCOME is the key in defining in sexual harassment. It is impact and effect the behaviour has on the recipient that will define the behaviour as sexual harassment.

What is a working? A workplace is any place where working relationships exist, where employer-employee relations exist.

Sexual Harassment: Prevention and Resolution

Combating Attitudes

Patriarchal attitudes and values are the biggest challenge in implementation of any law concerning women in our society. Combating these attitudes of men and women and the personnel involved/responsible for implementation of laws and systems is most crucial in prevention of unwanted sexual behaviour. Preventing and avoiding sexual harassment involves all leaves of employee/persons in any organization—employees and colleagues, management and bodies like trade unions. Most importantly it requires for the employer to act before a problem occurs. Steps employers can take to prevent sexual harassment. A policy/ procedure designed to deal with complaints of sexual harassment should be regarded as only one component to deal with the problem. The prime objective should be to change behaviour and attitudes, to seek to ensure the prevention of sexual harassment.

As an Employer Know the Following:

(i) First and foremost, acknowledge that it is your legal responsibility to provide safe working environment for women free from sexual harassment and discrimination and that you can be held liable for sexual harassment by employees.

(ii) Sexual harassment can have a devastating effect upon the health, confidence, morale and performance of those affected by it. The anxiety and stress produced by sexual harassment commonly leads to those subjected to it taking time off work due to sickness, being less efficient at work, or leaving their job to seek work elsewhere.

(iii) Understand the reasons why women remain silent about sexual harassment. An absence of complaints about sexual harassment does not necessarily mean absence of sexual harassment. It may mean that the recipients of sexual harassment think that there is no point in complaining because:
- nothing will be done about it;
- it will be trivialized;
- the complainant will be subjected to ridicule, or
- they fear reprisals.

(iv) Recognize the tangible and intangible expenses and losses organizations experience:

- costly investigation and litigation;
- negative exposure and publicity;
- embarrassing depositions;
- increased absenteeism;
- lowered employee morale;
- decreased efficiency;
- higher employee turnover;
- erosion of organisation's brand names, goodwill, and public image;
- negative impact on stock price.

The best way to prevent sexual harassment is to adopt a comprehensive sexual harassment policy. The aim is to ensure that sexual harassment does not occur and, where it does occur, to ensure that adequate procedures are readily available to deal with the problem and prevent its recurrence.

[I] Adopting Sexual Harassment Policy

What should be included in an anti-harassment policy? A basic policy should set forth the following:

1. An express commitment to eradicate and prevent sexual harassment and express prohibition of sexual harassment.
2. A definition of sexual harassment including both *quid pro quo* and hostile work environment giving examples.
3. An explanation of penalties (including termination) the employer will impose for substantiated sexual harassment conduct.
4. A detailed outline of the grievance procedure employees should use.
5. A clear statement that anyone found guilty of harassment after investigation will be subject to immediate and appropriate disciplinary action.

6. A clear understanding and strict rules regarding harassment of or by third parties like clients, customer, etc.
7. Additional resource or contact persons available for support and consultation.
8. An express commitment to keep all sexual harassment complaint and procedures confidential and time bound.
9. Provisions for training of employees at all levels.
10. An anti-retaliation policy providing protection against retaliation to complainants, witnesses, complaints committee member and other employees involved in prevention and complaints resolution.

Policies and procedures should be adopted after consultation or negotiation with employee's representatives. Experience suggests that strategies to create and maintain a working environment in which the dignity of employees is respected are most likely to be effective where they are jointly agreed.

[II] Communicate Policy

Issue a strong policy from the top authority against sexual harassment taking a 'zero tolerance' approach make sure it gets out to all employees either through the employee handbook or in memo form or with pay packets or with appointment letter. Have the employee sign it to acknowledge that they received and read the policy. The policy can also be posted in the workplace. If you have employees whose primary language is not English, have your sexual harassment policy translated or communicate to them in their primary language. Discuss the policy with all new employees ensure that third-party such as suppliers and customers are aware of your sexual harassment policy. Review the policy with your employees on regular basis.

[III] Enforce Policy

Take complaints of sexual harassment seriously and investigate all the sexual harassment charges quickly and thoroughly and professionally. Maintain accurate records of the investigation and the findings. Make sure employees who bring charges do not face retaliation ensure confidentially and time-bound response to complaints. Take immediate action when sexual harassment is discovered or suspected discpline appropriately any employee found to have engaged in sexual harassment. Safeguard your employees from third-party work-related sexual harassment.

Complaints Channel

Complaints channels need to provide different routes those employees can to file complaints, i.e. contacting the responsible authority for sexual harassment, a supervisor, calling a hotline, complaining through e-mail, etc. Organisations need to focus on the plight of the average individual. A policy is useless unless people use it, and most research indicate that a small fraction of employees ever say or do anything about harassing behaviour.

Informal methods of resolving complaints must be part of the complaints mechanism as 1. The objective is to end the harassing behaviour at the lowest possible (which is the most cost-effective, as well). 2. Many complaints can be resolved effectively and positively through informal methods. Informal options act as a buffer or filter, save bad blood, prevent the office environment getting uncomfortable for all, if employees can be advised as to how to handle the situation before it gets out of hands. Platforms to resolve complaints or to stop harassing behaviour must be provided before the complaints escalates into full-blown, formal complaints. The Supreme Court guidelines impose an obligation on the employer to set-up a complaints committee to deal with the cases of harassment. Such a committee should be headed by a woman, have half its members as women include a third-party representative from an NGO or any other agency conversant with the issue of sexual harassment (to prevent undue pressure from within the organization with respect to any complaint).

Complaints Committee

Employers need to set-up a redress mechanism/ complaints committees as per Vishaka Guidelines. First contact person from within the committee or otherwise should be appointed who could try to resolve the complaint informally first before the complaint goes to the formal channels of complaints committee. The organization needs to put down dearly, certain non-negotiable for the complaints committees for effective resolution of complaints.

Desired Qualities of the Members of Complaints Committee:

1. *Subjectively*—A sexual act when unwelcome is sexual harassment. The unwelcome is the women's subjective reality. The complaints committee's first job is to be believe in this reality, (unless something on record completely negates her complaints.
2. *Empathy*—The most important question to be answered in the affirmative that the committee and all functionaries must ask themselves while providing redress to a particular case is "Do well believe her?"

Other Steps Employees Can Take

Speaking Out

Speaking about sexual harassment is an effective tool in combating it. While speaking about it, the problem becomes visible, it is acknowledged that it exists, and this in turn leads one to take effective measure against it. Speaking about sexual harassment also gives an opportunity to clarify by this about it. It helps in changing attitudes a pepole towards this issue. Speaking about it creates enabling environment for the victim to speak out. It mobilises public opinion against it. It makes it difficult for a potential harasser to commit the crime. It equipes people with information as to what is to be done in such a case.

Speak up at the time: be sure to say 'NO' clearly, firmly and without smiling as that is the best way to let the harasser know that his behaviour is offensive. Objecting to the behaviour when it occurs helps if you decide to file charges later.

Keep Records

Keep track of what happens in a journal or diary and keep any letters or notes or other documents you receive. Write down the dates, times, places, and accounts of what happened. Write down the names of any witnesses. Write a letter. Pepole have successfully stopped sexual harassment by writing a letter detailing the behaviour that is offensive and punishing the person who is harassing them to stop the behaviour. The letter should be polite, unemotional, and detailed. Such a letter seems to be more powerful than a verbal request. The recipient of the letter seldom writes back, the persons usually just stops the behaviour.

Set your own boundaries: say 'NO' emphatically and clearly when you are asked to the places, do things, respond to questions, or engage in situation that make you uncomfortable. Do not worry about offending the other person or hurting his or her ego. Take care of your self first.

Be aware of situation and people who may harm you. Don't ignore others' warnings about particular people or social settings. Acknowledge their concern for you and for themselves.

Trust Your Own Inspects About Possible Danger

In an uncomfortable situation, be direct and honest and remove yourselves from the situation immediately. Regardless of your previous behaviour signals you may have given earlier, you have the absolute right to halt any sexual exchange at any time. Accept this write and act on it.

Tell Someone

Being quieter or stoic about sexual harassment lets it continue. Talk to other co-workers; you may be the only one harassed by this person. Do not blame yourselves and do not delay.

Create a Witness to the Behaviour

Inform a trusted colleague and try to insure that she is an eye or ear witness to a situation where you are being sexually harassed. This will be useful later if you chose to file a formal complaint. Send a copy of sexual harassment policy/rules to the harasser. If your workplace already has an anti-sexual harassment policy or the conduct rules of your institution prohibit sexual harassment, send a copy of the institution policy/conduct rules to the harasser with the appropriate sections underline.

Talk to the Union

If you are a member of a labour union, talk to your union representative.

Get a Medical Check-up

If you ahve been raped or physically assaulted, go for a medical check-up. Obtain a medical report. This is important, should you decide to pursue a legal case.

Report Sexual Harassment to the Appropriate Person in the Organization

Explore the different avenues available to you and file a formal complained if necessary. If your organization does not have a policy, and sure that your employer formulates an anti-sexual harassment policy and carries out all the connected tasks.

Documenting Harassment

Documenting the harassment is important for use as evidence in a case of complaint. You should photograph or keep copies of any offensive material at the workplace. Keep a journal with detailed information on instances or sexual harassment. Note the date conversations, Frequency of offensive and encounters, etc. obatin copies of your work records (including performance evaluations) and keep these copies at home also.

Other Documents that You Should Have

A company policy and proceed manual, these documents are very important to have. The companies documented policies on sexual harassment, discrimination performance appraisals, termination, affirmative action plans can be very important to show these stated policies versus there actions. Company newspapers, annual reports, pictures of its top executives, posters, company credo, company surveys are important to show the invaromebt and its hostility towards women.

Take all letters of recommendation, awards, thanks you's and anything at all that will corroborate your positive job performance. Pay special attention to documents that your superiors have provided lauding you and your work. If possible, ask your claints, staff, and peers for letters of commendation.

Every document that you use during trial must be authenticated by a witness. Keep this in mine your depositinwhent the defence Ask you were you optained a document. If you are not cleared about where you got the document, and who can authenticate it, you will not be able to use it during your trial.

The Gender Procedures: Sensitisation and People-friendly Police Project (KSP-UNICEF)

HAVING REGARD to the definition of 'human rights' in Section 2(d) of the Projection of Human Rights Act, 1993.

TAKING NOTE of the fact that the present civil and criminal laws in India do not adequately provide for specific protection of women from sexual harassment as workplaces and that enactment of such legislation will take considerable time.

It is necessary and expedient for employers in workplaces as well as other responsible persons or institutions to observe certain guidelines to ensure the prevention of sexual harassment of women.

1. **Duty of the Employer or other responsible persons in workplaces and other institutions:** It shall be the duty of the employers or other responsible persons or other institutions to prevent or deter the commission of acts of sexual harassment and to provide the procedures for the resolution, settlement or prosecution of acts, of sexual harassment by taking all steps required.
2. **Definition:** For this purpose, sexual harassment includes such unwelcome sexually determined behaviour (whether directly or by implication) as:
   (a) Physical contact advances;
   (b) A demand or request for sexual favours;
   (c) Sexually coloured remarks;
   (d) Showing pornography;
   (e) Any other unwelcome physical, verbal or non-verbal conduct of sexual nature.

Where any of these acts is committed in circumstances where under the victim of such conduct has a reasonable apprehension that in relation to the victim's employment or work she is drawing salary or honorarium or voluntary, whether in government, public or private enterprise such conduct can be humiliating and may constitute a health and safety problem. Its discriminatory for instance when the woman has reasonable grounds to believe that her objection would disadvantage her in connection with her employment or work including recruiting or promotion or when it creates a hostile work environment. Adverse consequences might be visited if the victim does not consent to the conduct in question or raises any objection thereto.

3. **Preventive Steps:** All employers or persons in-charge of workplace or private sector should take appropriate steps to prevent sexual harassment. Without prejudice to the generality of this obligation they should take the following steps:
   (f) Express prohibition of sexual harassment as defined above at the workplace should be notified, published and circulated in appropriate ways.
   (g) The rules/regulations of government and public sector bodies relating to conduct and discipline should include rules/regulations prohibiting sexual harassment and provide for appropriate penalties in such rules against the offender.
   (h) As regards private employers, steps should be taken to include the aforesaid prohibitions in the standing orders under the Industrial Employment (Standing Orders) Act, 1946.
   (i) Appropriate work conditions should be provided in respect of work, leisure, health and hygiene to further ensure that there is no hostile

environment towards women at workplaces and no employment.

4. **Criminal Proceedings:** Where such conduct amounts to a specific offence under the Indian Penal Code or under any other law, the employer shall initiate appropriate action in accordance with law by making a complaint with the appropriate authority.

In particular, it should ensure that victims, or witness are not victimized or discriminated against while dealing with complaints of sexual harassment. The victims of sexual harassment should have the option to seek transfer of the perpetrator or their own transfer.

5. **Disciplinary Action:** Where such conduct amounts to misconduct in employment as defined by the relevant service rules, appropriates disciplinary action should be initiated by the employer in accordance with those rules.
6. **Complaint Mechanism:** Whether or not such conduct constitutes an offence under law or a breach of the service rules, an appropriate complaint mechanism should be created in the employer's organization for redress of the complaint made by the victim. Such complaint mechanism should ensure time bound treatment of complaints.
7. **Complaints Committee:** The complaint mechanism, referred to in (6) above, should adequate to provide, where necessary, a Complaints Committee, a special counsellor or other support service, including the maintenance of confidentiality.

The Complaints Committee should be headed by a woman and not less than half of its member should be women. Further, to prevent the possibility of any undue pressure or influence from senior levels, such Complaints Committee should involve a third party, either NGO or other body who is familiar with the issue of sexual harassment.

The Complaints Committee must make an annual report to the government department concerned of the complaints and action taken by them.

The employers and person in-charge will also report on the compliance guidelines including on the reports of the government department.

Worker's Initiative: Employers should be allowed to raise issues of sexual harassment at a worker's meeting and in other appropriate forum and it should be affirmatively discussed in employer-employee meetings.

Awarness: Awareness of the rights of female employees in this regard should be created in particular by prominently the guidelines (and appropriate legislation when enacted on the subject) in a suitable manner.

8. **Third Party Harassment:** Where sexual harassment occurs as a result of an or omission by any third party or outside, the employer and person in-charge in will take all steps necessary and reasonable to assist the affected person in terms of support and preventive action.
9. The Central/State Governments are requested to consider adopting suitable measures including legislation to ensure that the guidelines laid down by this order also observed by the employers in private sector.
10. These guidelines will not prejudice any rights available under the Protection of Human Rights Act, 1993.

Other legal provisions include filling a criminal case under sections of the Indian Penal Code (IPC), the Indecent Representation of Women (Prohibition) Act and/or filling a civil suit.

The sections of the Indian Penal Code that can be applicable to sexual harassment (which makes it a criminal case):

1. Section 294

Whoever, to the annoyance of others, (a) does any obscene act in any public place, or (b) sings, recites and utters any obscene songs, ballads or words, in or near any public place, shall be punished with imprisonment of either description for a term that may extend to three months, or with fine, or with both.' This provisions is included in Chapter XVI entitles Of Offences Affecting Public Health, Safety, Convenience and Morals' and is cognizable, and triable by any magistrate.

2. Section 354

Whoever assaults or uses criminal force on any woman, intending to outrage her modesty or knowing it likely that he will therby outrage her modesty, shall be punished with imprisonment for a term which may extend to two years, or with fine, or with both.

3. Section 509

(Word, gesture or act intended to insult the modesty of a woman). This is included in Chapter 22 entitled 'Of Criminal Intimidation, Insult and Annoyance', and is cognizable, bailable and triable by any magistrate. It holds: "Whoever intending to insult the modesty of a woman, utters any word, makes any sound or gesture, or exhibits any object, intending that such word or sound shall be heard, or that such gesture is seen by such woman, or intrudes upon the privacy of such woman, shall be punished with simple imprisonment for a term which may extend to one year, or with fine, or with both."

Under the **Indecent Representation of Women (Prohibition) Act** (1987) if an individual harasses another with books, photographs, paintings, films, pamphlets, packages, etc. containing the "Indecent representation of women", they are liable for a minimum sentence of two years. Section 7 (Offenses by Companies) further holds companies where there has been 'indecent representation of women' (such as the display of pornography) on the premises, guilty of offenses under this act, with a minimum sectence of two years.

Civil Case

A civil suit can be filed for damages under tort laws. That is, the basis for filing the case would be mental anguish, physical harassment, loss of income and employment caused by the sexual harassment.

Threatening Atmosphere of Mutual Learning

Training for the members of the Complaints Committee and others who are going to be instrumental in implementing the policy is very essential. Their training should include a component of gender sensitization, along with the procedures for taking complaints, and for enquiry, etc.

Conduct yearly meetings with your supervisors to review the sexual harassment policy, and to make sure that they understand that an employee does not need to suffer negative consequences in order to make a complaint of sexual harassment. Inform the supervisors that even mild to moderate sexual jokes or statements can create an atmosphere of hostility that will make some employees uncomfortable, and could lead to the creation of a hostile working environment.

Sexual harassment training for all employees should address perceptions and understanding of sexual harassment, impact of sexual harassment, impact of sexual harassment on individuals and workplace, understanding the policy and complaints mechanism. The training for Complaints Committee should address, in addition to these. The procedures of investigation, skills necessary for enquiries, documenting the procedures.

Sensing Mechanism

Setting up a mechanism does not mean that there is sexual harassment in your workplace. Prevention is always better than cure, and being pro-active always helps. Along with performance, change in employee's behaviour patterns also deserves employer's close scrutiny.

Conducting Surveys — Conducting time-to-time surveys is helpful to identify and prevent factor/s situation leading to incidence of sexual harassment. The survey can be done anonymously and should be distributed with a copy of the companys sexual harassment policy. The survey can simply ask the employees (male and female) if they have experienced any form of sexual harassment during the past year. The survey also helps to show that the organization is actively engaged in preventing and correcting sexual harassment.

Commitment from Top

Commitment is shown through enforcement and action by the responsible authorities. Even the most comprehensive sexual harassment policies and procedures are bound to fall if a company does not enforce them quickly, consistently, and aggressively. To be effective, organizations must take sexual harassment seriously. They need certain that personnel responsible for enforcement conduct prompt, through, and documented investigations of all complaints, even those that appear trivial. Organizations should take action that is reasonably calculated to end the harassment. Such action must be directed toward the harasser and may include verbal warnings, written warnings, job transfers, suspension of employment, and if necessary termination.

Employers should also keep tabs on their supervisors. This can be accomplished by means of monthly meetings with higher management, unscheduled spot checks, or periodic sexual harassment training sessions with the implementing authorities.

Practices Consistent with Policies

Organizations must place just as much emphasis on reporting responsibilities and mechanisms as on the policy itself.

Setting a Precedence Even if the accused is a senior executive/a partner/any other person who is an asset to the company, and brings in a lot of business, it is essential that he must be punished if found guilty, as this sends out a strong message that the company will not tolerate any harassment by anyone.

What Steps can Employees Take to Prevent Sexual Harassment?

Most women themselves fail to recognizes sexual harassment and treat it as trivial and routine. Such has been the internal coping mechanism. Ignoring offensive behaviour or denying its existence are the most common ways women deal with sexual harassment.

In Back Off How To Confront and Stop Sexual Harassment and Harassment, Martha Langelan recommends taking these steps:—

Dealing with the Harasser Upfront

1. Do the unexpected: Name the behaviour. Whatever he's just done, say it, and be specific.
2. Hold the harasser accountable for his actions. Don't make excuses for him; don't pretend it didn't really happen. Take charge of the encounter and let people know what he did. Privacy protest harassers, but visibility undermines them.
3. Make honest, direct statements. Speak the truth (no threats, no insults, no obscenities, no appeasing verbal fluff and padding). Be serious, straightforward, and blunt.
4. Demand that the harassment stop.
5. Make it clear that all women have the right to be free from sexual harassment. Objecting to harassment is a matter of principle.
6. Stick to your own agenda. Don't respond to the harasser's excuses or diversionary tactics.
7. His behaviour is the issue. Say what you have to say, and repeat it if he persists.
8. Reinforce your statements with strong, self-respecting body language: eye contact, head up, shoulders back, a strong, serious stance. Don't smile. Timid, submissive body language will undermine your message.